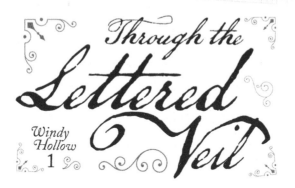

Through the Lettered Veil

Windy Hollow 1

CANDACE WEST

Through the Lettered Veil
© 2021 by Candace West
Lost Creek Press
Arkansas

ISBN: 978-0-578-30971-2

Scripture quotations are from the King James Version of the Bible.

Poem *Jesus Loves Me* by Anna Bartlett Warner quoted from the following work: Warner, Susan and Warner, Anna. *Say and Seal*. New York: J.B. Lippincott, 1860.

Cover Design: Roseanna White of Roseanna White Designs

WELCOME TO
THE MOSAIC COLLECTION

We are sisters, a beautiful mosaic united by the love of God through the blood of Christ.

Each month The Mosaic Collection releases one faith-based novel or anthology exploring our theme, Family by His Design, and sharing stories that feature diverse, God-designed families. All are contemporary stories ranging from mystery and women's fiction to comedic and literary fiction. We hope you'll join our Mosaic family as we explore together what truly defines a family.

If you're like us, loneliness and suffering have touched your life in ways you never imagined; but Dear One, while you may feel alone in your suffering—whatever it is—you are never alone!

Subscribe to *Grace & Glory*, the official newsletter of The Mosaic Collection, to receive monthly encouragement from Mosaic authors, as well as timely updates about events, new releases, and giveaways.

Learn more about The Mosaic Collection at
www.mosaiccollectionbooks.com

Join our Reader Community, too!
www.facebook.com/groups/TheMosaicCollection

If you'd like to find out about monthly launch team
opportunities, sign up at
www.mosaiccollectionbooks.com/launch-team

BOOKS IN
THE MOSAIC COLLECTION

When Mountains Sing by Stacy Monson
Unbound by Eleanor Bertin
The Red Journal by Deb Elkink
A Beautiful Mess by Brenda S. Anderson
Hope is Born: A Mosaic Christmas Anthology
More Than Enough by Lorna Seilstad
The Road to Happenstance by Janice L. Dick
This Side of Yesterday by Angela D. Meyer
Lost Down Deep by Sara Davison
The Mischief Thief by Johnnie Alexander
Before Summer's End: Stories to Touch the Soul
Tethered by Eleanor Bertin
Calm Before the Storm by Janice L. Dick
Heart Restoration by Regina Rudd Merrick
Pieces of Granite by Brenda S. Anderson
Watercolors by Lorna Seilstad
A Star Will Rise: A Mosaic Christmas Anthology II
Eye of the Storm by Janice L. Dick
Totally Booked: A Book Lover's Companion
Lifelines by Eleanor Bertin

PRAISE FOR CANDACE WEST

Civil War stories resonate with me for a number of reasons: they tell the story of our country's darkest hour and how the American Spirit of ingenuity, grit, and faith overcame. They bare the heart and soul of the conflicts that define us—a nation of ideals that forged a covenant with liberty and justice through the fires of sacrifice, hardship and grace.

In Candace West's newest historical, *Through the Lettered Veil*, these patriotic themes become personal in the struggle of Nolan, a Union soldier who returns home to his native Arkansas to face prejudice, lawlessness and injustice. His heroism not only seeks to win the tender-hearted Aynsley, but the stakes are much higher. A whole community besieged by vigilantism and violence hangs in the delicate balance of one man's will to summon the courage to confront evil, though he risks all.

In West's characteristically winsome writing voice, an epic story of courage triumphing over evil emerges. I found myself once again riveted and awed by the timeless truths communicated through her gift of story.

— KATHLEEN L. MAHER, award winning author of the Sons of the Shenandoah Series

Betrayals stem from jealousy and consequences of poor choices. Civil War allegiances pit brother against brother. Parent against child. Neighbor against neighbor. Families and communities pay the ultimate price. In Through the Veiled Letters Candace West weaves a moving story of forgiveness, redemption, and renewal amidst the anger and vengeance consuming this Ozark Mountain community. You'll love Aynsley and Nolan and cheer for them to the end.

— LYNN U. WATSON, Author of *Cinnamah Brosia's Inspirational Collection for Women: The Essence of Courage, The Essence of Joy,* and *The Essence of Humility*

ACKNOWLEDGMENTS

Above everything, all glory goes to my Lord and Savior Who inspires me with these stories and helps me overcome my limitations.

My heartfelt thanks belongs to my family and my fantastic reader friends who delight me with their encouraging words and friendship. All of you bless me beyond measure. I pray my stories uplift you in the same way.

Thank you, Kathy Maher, for cheering on my stories. I pinch myself every time I've received an endorsement and thank the Lord for your friendship. I wish we lived closer because I know we'd have a blast together, exploring historical places. If you're ever near Vicksburg, give me a call!

A shout out belongs to my fellow Mosaic sister Sara Davison for her vicious edits! Thank you for pointing out the rough patches and embarrassing mistakes. Your gracious spirit will not go unrewarded in God's kingdom.

I send lots of hugs to my other sets of eyes, Lynn Watson and Eileen Ward. Your input is invaluable. Thank you for taking time to read this story and make it better.

Not least of all, I send my love and gratitude to all of my Mosaic sisters. Getting to know you is a pleasure, and I always look forward to our Zoom meetings. You help me keep my faith in humanity. Each of you is a treasure, and I'm humbled that you invited me to be part of the family. Camry, you are an author's angel. Thank you for all the tireless work you do to introduce our stories to readers.

For Aunt Joyce Eddlemon Blake, who is a living testimony of courage and joy

CHAPTER ONE

May 1865
Arkansas Ozarks

Aynsley's high collar tightened around the knot forming in her throat. Against the window, rain splattered into thousands of pieces, much like her throbbing heart. She twisted the lace handkerchief between her fingers, choosing her next words carefully.

"Are you quite sure these are accurate?"

"Miss O'Brien, I assure you, he wrote this three weeks ago." Uncle Stewart's lawyer, Mitchum Kirby, leaned back in his chair, the wooden spindles creaking beneath his middle-age weight.

Air whooshed from Aynsley's lungs. She must remain composed. Her upbringing, years of training, demanded it, especially since Uncle was barely cold in his grave. Dear Uncle Stewart! Pain like a dull knife dug further into her heart.

Despite her upbringing, she pushed her chair from the desk and paced the office floor. The early springtime chill seeped through her shoes and crawled up her legs. The dying fire crackling on the hearth did little to warm the room.

"How dare he. He never breathed a word, never once hinted. Did he ever explain his reasons?" Her usually placid voice rose and shook.

Kirby sighed, impatience digging into the corners of his mouth. "He never explained, but the reason is obvious."

Aynsley slammed her eyes shut against the echo in her mind—the discharge of a pistol that had robbed Uncle Stewart of his life. She halted. "What did you say the terms were?"

Kirby quirked an eyebrow, gesturing a hand over the papers on the desk. "Thirty days or you forfeit the property."

"You mean my inheritance." Aynsley ground her teeth. From the time she was a little girl, Uncle Stewart had trained her to control her temper. Her fiery, short outbursts had gotten her into more than a few scrapes. So much he often despaired she would ever be ladylike as tradition and her upbringing required. She thought, however, she had mastered it quite well.

Until now.

She took a deep, shuddering breath and counted the way Aunt Eva had taught her, God rest her soul. One. Two. Three. Four. Five. She exhaled.

"I cannot give up Windy Holler. Surely you understand, Mr. Kirby."

As he rubbed his brown mustache, a twinge of pity softened his firm expression. "It matters none if I do or not, Miss O'Brien. The fact remains you must marry within thirty days, or you lose everything but ten acres with your grandfather's house. It was your uncle's express wish that you marry."

"And if I don't?"

"I've read it twice. Here it is." He held up the stack. "Everything is there."

Those papers, held out to her, doused her temper as though Kirby had thrown icy spring water on her. She stared. Nothing petrified Aynsley more than written words. Only her family had known.

"I was too upset and shocked when you read it. Please read it once more."

Kirby shook his head. He thumbed through the stack until he found the page.

"If, within thirty days, Aynsley O'Brien fails to procure a husband, all ownership of property will transfer to Elnora O'Brien Howard. The ten acres originally belonging to William O'Brien will remain within Aynsley O'Brien's possession."

Aynsley's eyes slid closed. "When does my time begin?"

"A week from the date of your uncle's death." Four days had passed.

"I'm in mourning."

Once more, Kirby shuffled the papers. "I believe your welfare was more important to him than your mourning."

Uncle's voice whispered clearly in her mind. His last words. *Darlin', forgive me. One day—*

His hand, grasping hers, had slackened as he slipped away from her. His blue eyes dulled. Vacant.

A thousand hot pinpricks stung her eyelids. Aynsley jerked a lace-trimmed handkerchief from the pocket of her skirt. Her trembling hands pressed it against her eyes, stemming the breach of tears that threatened to fall. Not here, especially while Kirby's voice was dragging her thoughts to the present.

"I'm sorry." She sucked in another breath and straightened her shoulders. "You were saying?"

"Perhaps in a few days, when you've adjusted to the idea, you'll see that your uncle has your best interests at heart."

Heat flamed into Aynsley's cheeks. "I believe I know what is in my best interest. After all, I am twenty-two. A veritable prickly old maid."

Kirby's gray eyes appraised her from the top of her glossy, black hair to the hem of her black mourning dress. So intent was his stare, in fact, that Aynsley wondered if a lock of her hair was out of place. She returned the stare, daring him to argue further.

"You are indeed. Twenty-two, I mean." Breaking eye contact, he turned to the final page and laid it on her side of the desk. "There's one thing more. You must sign here, acknowledging you agree to the terms of the will."

"And if I don't?"

"Then you'll forfeit the property immediately to Elnora."

Her cousin, Uncle Stewart's daughter, resided in Vicksburg, having no use for the farm. Like a heavy, wool cloak, despair wrapped around Aynsley and curled at her feet. She was cornered. Either sign or lose everything. Aynsley stepped forward, no longer feeling the chilly, spring air. A gaping, black hole swallowed every emotion of her heart.

Sitting once more, she watched Kirby dip the fountain pen in the ink. Then her eyes skittered to the bottom of the page where she would sign her name.

"Miss O'Brien?"

Save for her clenched jaw, Aynsley composed her face and took the pen from Kirby's waiting fingers. Before putting it to paper, she bent her head and closed her eyes as she had been trained and made the swift strokes of her name. Once finished, she opened her eyes.

The letters from her signature seemed to tumble around the page. Blinking, Aynsley glanced up, resisting the urge to shake her head. Refocused.

To keep Windy Holler, she had signed away her life.

In the corner, the clock chimed two. What had she done?

"Is there anything else?" She hated the sound of her small and defeated voice.

"For the moment, no." With deft fingers, Kirby stacked the papers and set them aside. "If I can be of any more assistance, drop by anytime."

Clamping her lips, Aynsley rose without bothering to answer and opened the door. She stepped into the entryway and banged the door shut harder than necessary.

Eleazar, the overseer of Windy Holler, stood and waited. Avoiding his questioning gaze, she strode over to the hat rack and plucked up her bonnet. She settled it on her head and tied it under her chin, careful to keep her back to him. The magnitude of her decision seized Aynsley. Her fingers froze.

"You ready, ma'am?"

His deep, rich voice, so full of kindness and sympathy, nearly burst the barriers of her restraint.

"Miss Aynsley?"

She cleared her throat and turned, schooling her expression. "Yes. I'm ready."

"The rain's let up. Looks like the worst has passed." Eleazar nodded toward the window and handed her the umbrella.

"Has it, Eleazar?"

His muddy, brown eyes, the color of the Mississippi, gleaned understanding from hers. "Only the Good Lord knows for sure."

Holding her skirts away from the puddled, grassless path, Aynsley scrutinized the two-story cabin with its central dogtrot, as folks in those parts called it. Chickens, dogs, or other critters could meander through the airy space—within reason. In other places, it was known as a breezeway.

The steep, wood-shingled roof stretched from the upper, open landing to the front porch below, casting a wide shadow over the chickens pecking around the steps. Windy Holler had been her home for as long as she could remember, built by Uncle Stewart.

The coal-gray sky dimmed windows that usually sparkled in the sunlight. In happier times, it reminded her of someone trying to hide a laugh. Almost as though the house felt the joy within its walls. Now, it brooded at her.

Aynsley climbed the steps. Damp, cool air feathered across her cheeks. A silent touch of times past. Like the four soulless, silent rooms waiting for her downstairs and upstairs.

Perhaps this is what Uncle Stewart meant. He knew she would be all alone here with Eleazar and his wife, Becca. Unprotected. Her bonnet strings choked her.

Deep inside, Aynsley's heart rebelled, to no avail. The war had ravaged the Ozarks. Though the main thrust of the Union and Confederate armies had maneuvered around the rugged terrain with few battles, the guerrillas scourged the hills like wildfire. Bushwhackers and Jayhawkers alike. No one was safe—not man, woman, or child.

Uncle Stewart, with the help of local home guards, fought to protect his family and neighbors from the merciless and bloodthirsty Confederates and Unionists. No family had come through the last four years unscathed.

And still, war hovered on her doorstep, threatening to destroy all she held dear.

After entering the parlor, Aynsley placed her drawstring bag on a chair and wandered to the window. She scanned the bare room, at one time graced with heirlooms and furnishings lost to the clutches of marauders. Truly, the remaining beds and chairs seemed a luxury.

They'd learned to let them raid their stores rather than attempt to stop them. Uncle Stewart displayed restraint whenever they barged into their home, taking things at will. To keep from starving, they had built a false wall in the cellar and stored food out of sight.

Parting the curtain, Aynsley scanned the bare fields, their early spring undergrowth peeking from beneath fallow soil. The best bottom soil in the valley, elevated enough to avoid the floods yet level and rich. Grandfather had chosen well when settling the land.

During the war, it had been their curse. Their yield had mostly filled the bellies of men whose allegiance was to themselves, leaving little for their family.

A cold judder raced down Aynsley's spine. Looking to the east, she spied the charred remnants of the barn. A token from Uncle Stewart's murderers.

"Lord, forgive me for hating those who have tormented us," she hissed.

Ashes and danger lay in wait for her. Mr. Kirby had spoken truthfully. The reasons for Uncle Stewart's demands struck her like a slap. The bonds of matrimony would shield her from desperate men. A young woman possessing fertile farmland was an easy target for the ruthless displaced by the war.

Another shudder tremored through her, but this time, the memories stemmed from another source.

"How far am I willing to go?" She grasped the window sill. The thought of binding herself to any man, except one, rankled. And he wanted nothing to do with her.

Perhaps letting Windy Holler go to Elnora was for the best. Could she stand it here without Uncle Stewart and Aunt Eva, the two people she loved most in the world?

Something within her died.

CHAPTER TWO

Sparse remains of the split-rail fence bordered the yard. From the shaded corner of the long front porch, a hound bared his teeth, a low, menacing rumble deep in his chest. Nolan Scottsdale raised a stained glove and shaded his eyes. Yep, it was Ol' Hickory, all right. Older and more raw-boned, the dog's yellow eyes glittered a warning not to be ignored. Hickory never bluffed. After four years, would the dog remember him?

Nolan whistled low. "Hickory, boy."

Hickory's ears pricked, and he jogged forward as the front door thrust open, arresting his steps. A middle-aged lady crossed the threshold, cradling a rifle in the crook of her arm.

"What business do you have here? Yanks aren't welcome."

Swallowing gritty road dust, Nolan shifted on the saddle and removed his hat. "Mother, it's me."

Viola Borden squinted, her face blanching. "Nolan?" Her voice wobbled. Azure eyes raked the length of his faded blue uniform. "You're either brave or very foolish to show up in these parts wearing that garb."

"It's all I have."

"You'll get nothing from here."

"I'm not looking for anything except work."

"You won't find that here either."

Nolan tightened his fingers around the reins. Four years hadn't doused his mother's anger at him for choosing the opposite side. He flicked a glance around the place. "The condition of the farm tells another story. The fence needs mending, and the fields are bare. Mother, I'd like to put things behind us and start fresh. Let me help."

A ripple of yielding smoothed the premature crow's feet around Mother's eyes, but her mouth remained firm. "Daniel is capable of doing the job. He's eighteen."

Nolan's half-brother had been a boy of fourteen when the war began. He'd forgotten that Daniel was a young man. "I'm not looking to take his place, just to do an honest day's work and have a place to lay my head. Even if it's in the barn."

"We'll get by."

Mother knew how to dig in her heels. Nolan spied a large vegetable garden tucked almost out of sight behind the house, nearly at the back door.

She followed his stare. "We've had our share of thieving vermin these years. We grow the food close and keep watch. This place ain't the same as you remember."

Nolan frowned. "Where's Papa?" Surely his stepfather would convince Mother to let him stay. Through the years, he'd been a buffer between them.

Mother's face hardened like cold granite. "He's dead."

A sharp intake of breath hissed between Nolan's lips, and he lurched over the saddle horn as though someone had punched him. "Dead? When did he die?"

"Two years this spring."

Two years. The only father Nolan had ever known had been gone from earth, and he never knew it. He shook his head, dispelling the clamor of his thoughts. "Why didn't you tell me?"

"You were gone fighting. The day you left, I told you not to expect a word from me." Mother swiped a strand of limp, golden hair from her cheek. "Do you have any idea what we've been through? Both sides like the devil himself. Folks robbed, bushwhacked, or starved. Your papa was bushwhacked 'cause you took sides with the Yanks." She shifted her rifle. "Your five brothers and I took turns keeping watch after that, day and night. They torched our barn."

"But our family was neutral."

"There's no neutrality in war." Mother moved to go inside. "Get rid of those clothes, Captain, or they'll be digging your grave next."

The door shut, and the sound of a bolt slid into place, effectively locking Nolan out of his home.

Before grief could snag him, Nolan turned his horse and headed down the grassy lane. Moisture stung his eyes, and he swiped a sleeve across them. Papa bushwhacked because of him.

Lord, forgive me.

Overhead, the birds twittered in the branches, a sound he often dreamed of during long nights of homesickness. The birdsong mocked him now. Papa had been a kind, gentle man, marrying Nolan's widowed mother and adopting him when he was two years old.

Though Mother gave him more sons in the following years, Thomas Borden treated Nolan as flesh and blood. He never censured Nolan for joining the Union but promised his prayers would go with him. On cold nights, the memory of Papa's warm handclasp bidding him farewell had bolstered Nolan's waning courage.

And not one note from Mother telling him of Papa's passing. Nolan clenched his jaw and glanced down at his dusty uniform. The musty, pungent odor of days traveling home collided into his nose, blotting out the fresh scent of the woods and wildflowers.

Where was he to go? Mother was right. He had to dispose of the uniform. Strange, but he wouldn't be sorry to rid himself of it. He'd had enough fighting and bloodshed. The screams of dying men on the battlefield roared in his ears. Perhaps even here in the hills Nolan loved, he would find no rest. Home was barred to him. He should've known. Once Mother set her mind, only Heaven could move it.

Nolan pressed his knees into the sides of his Morgan mount, easing the horse into a lope. A burning pain in his right thigh seared down to his toes. Almost three years ago, he'd suffered a wound which came close to taking his leg. The sounds of battle crowded his thoughts, but he shoved them aside and focused on the road.

"What are we to do, Thunder?"

Alert to every sound, the steed snorted. Nolan thought of his former friends and neighbors but doubted they would give him a place to stay. Though many supported the Union cause, they weren't anxious to invite trouble. He'd heard of the marauders.

After a mile, the land leveled into a valley of open fields. He was nearing O'Brien land.

Nolan's chest cinched. How had they fared? Was Aynsley among the living? Dared he broach the barrier between them if she were?

Of all people, the O'Briens might extend a hand to him. Their allegiance to the Union was unwavering.

At least, in the beginning. What damage had four years of war done?

Beads of sweat prickled between Aynsley's shoulder blades as she climbed the back steps of the house. The walk to the spring had failed to clear her mind of its worries.

As Aynsley hung her bonnet on a peg, Becca's soft footfalls approached from the kitchen. An outspoken abolitionist, Uncle Stewart had hired Eleazar and Becca, both free, to protect them from capture and enslavement. Freedom papers meant nothing to dishonest men.

Aynsley remembered peeking from behind Aunt Eva's skirt at the dark man and woman when they first entered the house. Since that time, the man and his wife had won their trust as fellow laborers and friends.

"Ma'am," Becca whispered, her hushed voice barely reaching Aynsley's ears.

Aynsley frowned. "What's wrong, Becca?"

"You have a caller. He's been waitin' almost half an hour."

Without bothering to clamp down on a sigh, Aynsley put her hands on her hips. "Who is it?"

"Nolan Scottsdale."

Shock slammed into her ribs. "Nolan?" She cut a glance toward the closed parlor door. "Did he say what he wanted?"

"No, ma'am. Just that he wanted to see you."

Aynsley bit her lip. Nolan Scottsdale hadn't wanted to see her in four years. "I suppose there's nothing to do but to see him. Thank you, Becca." Squaring her shoulders, Aynsley composed her face and stepped toward the door. With every step, her heart thudded harder.

She took a breath and twisted the doorknob. Taking her time, she stepped over the threshold and shut the door before glancing his way.

Nolan stood at the fireplace, his hands clasped behind him. As he pivoted toward her, she lifted her chin.

Same wavy golden hair, same nose with a slight, imperceptible crook—the result of a fall from an apple tree

24

when he was ten. Same piercing blue eyes making her feel as though she could never hide anything from him. To her misfortune, she had.

Road dust clung to every inch of his blue uniform, a bit worse for wear.

"Mr. Scottsdale, it's nice to see you again." The lie tasted thick and bitter on her tongue.

Nolan's keen glance flicked over her, no hint of a smile on his lips. "Miss O'Brien," he drawled blandly, as though they'd hadn't shared most of their lives. He tipped his head, nodding slightly. "I asked to see Mr. O'Brien, but Becca told me of his recent passing as well as your aunt's last year." His cool blue eyes warmed a touch. "They were good people, good friends. I'm sorry for your loss."

Oh, not that. Not kind words, not his sympathy. Rebuffing his aloof attitude with anger was easy, but his kindness would split her aching heart. Better to hide in resentment.

"Thank you," her stiff lips managed.

"Is there anything I can do?"

"No." Aynsley resisted the urge to whisk a wayward lock of hair from her forehead. "I'm sorry I kept you waiting. Aren't you with the cavalry?"

Only then did Nolan break his rigid posture. "I was discharged two weeks ago."

Raising her eyebrows, Aynsley waited.

Nolan cleared his throat and ran a hand through his roguish waves. An unconscious habit betraying his nervousness. How she remembered.

He worked his jaw as though the next words irked him. "I came to talk business with your uncle, but I suppose you'll do."

She'd do? Aynsley narrowed her eyes. "Business? Can't it wait?"

Nolan shook his head. "I'm afraid not. Believe me, I don't

like this any more than you, but I might as well be honest. I'm unwelcome at home. I wanted to help work the farm, but I'm not needed."

The air thickened around her head. A dizzying, sickening feeling knotted in the pit of her stomach. Aynsley was well acquainted with Mrs. Borden's sharp tongue and hardened demeanor.

Nolan glanced at the window. "I noticed the barren fields as I entered the valley."

"Times are lean, Mr. Scottsdale. Because of the raids on our harvests, we did well to maintain large vegetable gardens. We guarded them 'round the clock and hid our stores, keeping enough in sight to satisfy the thieves. Our barn was recently burned down."

"I'm sorry."

For a long, silent moment, they contemplated each other. Was he remembering their good times? She cleared her throat. "You mentioned business. What could I possibly do?"

"I need a job."

Aynsley crossed her arms. "What kind?"

"Let me farm the land. I raise the crops, and we share the profits. With Eleazar's help, we can do it."

Could this day go any more wrong? A demand to marry followed by a business proposal from an old friend turned into a hostile stranger. Aynsley's head ached.

"Your offer comes at the worst possible time."

"How so? Your land is in desperate need of farming, and you'll need provisions as well as the income."

"You're telling me?" Aynsley crossed to the sofa and dropped onto the cushion. With her fingertips, she kneaded her forehead. "Excuse me. I've had a difficult day."

"The loss of your uncle is no doubt a heavy weight."

"It's more than that. Uncle Stewart has cornered me." She

gestured toward a chair. "Please sit. I must be honest with you."

Though a flicker of suspicion narrowed Nolan's eyes, he sat on the armchair, his posture rigid.

Since she couldn't bear to meet his eyes, Aynsley focused on the oak leaf hooked rug in the center of the floor. The intricate colors and beauty demonstrated the long hours Aunt Eva had labored over it. The lingering beauty of her home. Uncle Stewart had said t'was a shame for feet to trod it.

"Miss O'Brien?"

Inwardly, she bristled over his formal use of her name. Twisting her fingers in her lap, she kept her head down. "Uncle Stewart left the property, everything, to me. Elnora lives in Vicksburg. She has no need of it, though her husband recently died. However, my uncle left one stipulation in the will. I must comply, or I will forfeit all of the property except my grandfather's original ten acres and his cabin."

Nolan shifted on the seat. "What does he require?"

"I'm loathe to say. It's humiliating, really, but you need to know why I can't accept your business proposition. I have thirty days to comply. It's pointless for you to break ground and start a crop when I'll lose it all."

"You sound like you've made up your mind not to comply."

"I don't see how I can."

"It can't be as bad as all that. Your uncle doted on you."

"I assure you, it is very bad."

"What is it?"

Gripping her fingers tighter, Aynsley counted the rose petals in the center of the rug. "I must marry within thirty days or lose it all."

Nolan sprang from the chair, his tall frame casting a long shadow across the rug. "Marry? Are you engaged?"

As she ventured a glance, Aynsley's cheeks burned. "No."

Nolan swallowed. "The idea is foolish at best and unkind at worst."

"At least we agree on that."

"Why would he do it?"

"An unprotected, unmarried woman owning property will lure every no-good straggler looking for a place to roost. And some closer than you think." Aynsley's throat cramped with the thought of one such person.

Nolan's chest expanded and fell. "The war has made savages out of a lot of men. I'm sorry to have troubled you. I'll see myself out."

"Wait." Aynsley rose. "I'm assuming you have no place to stay."

A slow, wry smile curved Nolan's mouth. "None. I never should've left Virginia."

"My grandfather's cabin is empty except for a few furnishings. There is a bed. We always keep it clean, though it does need repairs. You're welcome to remain there until you find a place."

The smile gentling his features vanished like a snuffed-out candle. "I don't wish to impose or be beholden to anyone."

"You mean me." Aynsley cringed. "You're a soldier, and you've done a hard, costly duty to our country. I can't imagine the hardships you've suffered, but I'm grateful. If anyone is beholden, it's me. The cabin is yours to use, if you wish."

Blinking, Nolan rubbed his chin, his jangled thoughts almost audible to Aynsley. "Sunset isn't far off. I suppose I can stay one night. Thank you."

"It's nothing, really. I'll speak with Becca. We'll fix food for you. Eleazar will take you there and help ready things. Stay as long as you need, Mr. Scottsdale."

A glimmer of irritation ticked Nolan's jaw. Perhaps he didn't like her formal use of *his* name. Gathering her skirts, Aynsley brushed past him and called Becca.

CHAPTER THREE

Filthy bath water smacked the grass and splattered the rock foundation of William O'Brien's cabin. Nolan hung the tin washtub on a peg beside the back door and smoothed the hem of his fresh trousers, three inches too short at the ankles. Straightening, he closed his eyes and let the evening breeze cool his temples.

The bath had nearly made him feel like a new man, scouring away days of hard travel. Guilt nipped the edges of his conscience when he glanced at the clean shirt and pants, courtesy of Aynsley's uncle. The shirt constricted his movements, and the buttons stretched the holes to the point of ripping the cloth. However, they were clean, and he was grateful for them. In the morning, the thick scruff on his face would meet the same fate as the bathwater soaking the ground.

In the distance, a shadow caught Nolan's eyes. The silhouette of a dainty head and dress trudged up a grassy hill toward the O'Brien graveyard. No doubt Aynsley was paying her respects, shrouding her grief under the cover of twilight.

Aynsley. A name passing his lips during the early, waking

hours of a dream, carrying him to afternoons in the O'Brien's apple orchard where he and she played chase. With the passing years, childhood romps had morphed into afternoon rambles in the fields as they swapped dreams. At one time, he dared believe they shared the same dream.

Despite the years and contention between them, Nolan yearned to follow and share her troubles. She had effectively shut him out, though. No matter how far he'd traveled, nor how many battles had raged, nothing had quenched his love for her. Neither fire nor flood. Nor hungry nights and days in the saddle. He would never be free.

While she remained unbound. Her polite, impersonal letter to him had dashed all hope when he left to join the Union. After enlisting, he had summoned enough courage to profess his feelings in a letter and ask Aynsley to wait for him. When no answer came, he wrote two more.

Groaning, Nolan ran a hand through his damp hair. Finally, her letter had come. He'd ripped into it, certain of the answer. Had he not often sensed her feelings when they ambled the evenings away in O'Brien's orchard?

Her words shattered everything but his devotion. How he wished it had.

Though I hold you in the deepest regard, I could never promise my heart.

Aynsley reached the graveyard gate, and Nolan stalked away from the sight. A spasm rocked his thigh, worsening his limp as he climbed the steps and entered the cabin.

I'm a fool for coming here.

Save for Eleazar and Becca, she was alone and defenseless, in need of help. He was a homeless soldier, an outcast among his family. Come dawn, the sunrise would warm his retreating back as Thunder carried him to friendlier places. Did he possess the courage to ride away?

Did he have the nerve to stay?

Weariness and the burden of leaving Aynsley to fend for herself whirled Nolan's thoughts like wind stirring embers. Shuffling to one corner of the room where the rope bed stood, he knelt and propped his elbows on the cotton ticking. The unforgiving, hard floor pressed against his knees. The gnawing in his heart proved more painful.

Bending his head, Nolan moved his lips in prayer. Though he was exhausted, sleep wouldn't claim him tonight.

Sitting in a chair, Aynsley stared through the window pane while the moon steadily rose over the Ozarks. The walk to the graveyard had seemed especially long this time. Beneath the folds of her nightgown, her legs ached, but her core panged the worst.

Though Nolan often visited through the realm of dreams, she hadn't expected to see him again. Try as she might, she had failed to banish the image of him in his dirty uniform. The tousled hair and heavy, reddish stubble. The weary shadows under his eyes. Premature crow's feet digging around them. Yet, beneath all of it, Aynsley spied the man she loved.

Though the evening was warm, she shivered and rubbed her upper arms. Theirs had been a forbidden friendship. Mrs. Borden had harbored an intense dislike for Aynsley, the reason unclear to her and Nolan.

But that hadn't stopped him.

At school, after chores, or on Sunday afternoons between church meetings, he found ways to seek her out. Long ambles in the apple orchard often ended with Nolan reading to her.

Aynsley touched her palm against her cheek, remembering. Of all the things they shared, she'd never summoned the courage to confess her inability to read. Her weak-mindedness.

Nolan was intelligent, keen, and had planned to become a doctor. Though she could never measure up to him, she had displayed a clever, quick-witted front, internally cramming down her shame.

Elnora's haughty face threatening to tell Nolan flashed through Aynsley's thoughts, filling her again with dread.

"Not now." Casting the memories aside, Aynsley shoved herself from the chair and shuffled to the trunk at the foot of the bed. She stared at its rounded top. Many of her dreams resided there, shuttered, only revisited in quiet, reflective moments.

She knelt and raised the lid. The smell of fabric, paper, and dried flowers flitted like kind phantoms, the smell of happier times. Sifting through the girlish mementos, Aynsley pulled three envelopes from beneath her mother's dresses.

Glancing at the address, she recognized her name before the rest of the words started swimming. Nolan's letters to her after he enlisted. She closed her eyes. Though she couldn't read them, the contents were inscribed on her heart.

He had suspected her feelings for quite a while and dreaded to broach the subject. "Though I hold you in the deepest regard, you will always be a dear sister to me," Aynsley whispered. "Let us not spoil our friendship with impossible dreams."

Under the cover of night, she had watered her pillow for weeks. The other two letters expressed his heartfelt concern for her, especially since she hadn't answered. Aynsley hadn't seen the need. Besides, to ask Elnora or Aunt Eva to write her response would have been worse than humiliating.

The last letter stung the worst. "I will trouble you no further. It pains me to lose a friendship I counted as one of the best I have ever known. I pray you find happiness, Aynsley."

He'd severed their friendship with the flourish of a pen. The troubles she'd endured in the following four years should've hardened her heart to his words, to him. "I thought it had." Aynsley thrust the envelopes into their place and snapped the lid shut.

Anger rumbled against her ribs, a spasm worse than loneliness. How dare he show up with the audacity to ask for help? She should've thrown him out.

"Forgive me, Lord. What am I thinking?" Standing, she returned to the chair and slumped onto it. "Have I become heartless?" She lowered the wick of the kerosene lamp on the side table. The flame flickered and snuffed into darkness.

Near the charred barn, Aynsley saw Eleazar walking the perimeter of the grounds, holding a gun, his posture alert for the slightest unnatural sound. He rose every few hours at night, checking for signs of trouble. Beside him trotted Duke their faithful cur, ready to spring into motion at the slightest command. The years had sharpened him as well.

Through the window, the moonlight streamed into the room, spilling around Aynsley's bare feet. So strange, moonlight. Unlike the sun's rays, it offered no warmth. Neither did it chill. It glazed everything, its sheen belonging to another world.

So thin hung the veil between present and past, between understanding and questioning. In daylight, she banished the questions like one might dispel dust and continued the business of living, moving through the grief.

But at night.

Aynsley bent her head. "Father, I ask You to guide me to make the right decision. Should I comply with Uncle Stewart's request or let Windy Holler fall into Elnora's hands?"

The latter made Aynsley's blood run cold.

CHAPTER FOUR

"Good morning, Miss O'Brien."

Aynsley dropped the remaining handful of clothes into the boiling pot and grabbed a wooden paddle to stir them. "Good morning, Mr. Scottsdale. This is wash day. It'll be quite a while before your uniform is ready, though I advise against wearing it."

"I've already been warned. I reckon for now I'll hide in your uncle's duds."

Hide, indeed. Through the rising steam, she flicked a glance over the tight shirt covering Nolan's muscles and the too-short trousers. Her eyes scanned his clean-shaven face. "You might be mistaken for a carpetbagger instead." She resisted the urge to smirk.

Nolan grimaced. "The thought crossed my mind.

"I'm sorry there's nothing else I can do." Aynsley stirred the clothes.

"Maybe there is. Could I have a word in private?"

Dabbing an arm over her clammy forehead, Aynsley stepped away from the pot. "Becca, would you mind taking over for a bit?"

"No, ma'am. You and Mr. Nolan go on ahead." A smile parted her lips.

Rolling down the cuffs of her blouse, Aynsley joined Nolan as he turned toward the orchard. Unwanted emotions toyed with her heart. She must make their conversation brief.

"What is it, Mr. Scottsdale?"

Nolan jammed his hands into his pockets. "I've been studying on your problem."

His jaw ticked, and a guilty prick of satisfaction twinged Aynsley.

"Oh?"

"To be honest, I didn't sleep a wink for thinking and praying on it."

"It isn't your problem."

"The way I see it, it's our problem. Besides that, I need work, an income."

"What of your plans to become a doctor?"

Nolan released a long breath between his lips as if letting something go. "It's too late. The war stole my chance. Time to make the best of what's left."

"I'm sorry, truly."

Nolan shrugged. "It's no matter. The trouble is you need a husband, and I need Windy Holler."

Aynsley halted, her shoes digging into the grass. "What are you saying?"

Nolan turned, his stare boring into hers. "Marry me."

Gasping, she staggered backwards several steps, outraged. "You can't be serious!"

"I assure you, I've never been more serious."

"But you said—" she sputtered, recalling his letters. Catching herself, she clamped her lips shut.

"Please don't misunderstand. This is a business contract between us. Nothing more."

"But ... but marriage?"

"What other choice do you have?"

Gritting her teeth, Aynsley curled her fingers into fists. "None."

"Exactly." Nolan rocked on his heels, no doubt emphasizing his point.

"Marriage is a lifetime contract."

"I'm well aware. Why do you think I didn't sleep?"

Aynsley's skirts swirled around her ankles as she headed for the washpot. A warm, restraining hand closed around her arm.

"You could do worse." A glimmer of humor deepened his voice, and she braced herself against it. No, she could never do better than him.

She tugged her arm, to no avail. "I prefer to remain as I am."

"If you do, you'll lose everything but ten acres and a crude cabin."

Shooting a glare, she lifted her chin. "And what do you have to gain?"

"Everything."

What a nondescript answer, so like a man. His blue eyes clashed into hers with an unspoken challenge. Standing this close to him weakened her defenses.

She yanked her arm once more. "Let go of me."

Immediately, Nolan dropped his hand, and she shrank a few steps away, ignoring the regret in her traitorous heart.

"I hope you'll consider my offer seriously. I daresay you can't trust anyone else who might offer to marry you. You have nothing to fear from me. You'll have an equal part of everything."

Nolan was right, as always. He was a man of his word. As silence stretched between them, his stare darkened. "I'm looking out for my interests, to be sure, but yours come first."

The air around her head buzzed. She needed to sit down

and quick. Resisting the urge to gulp, she fumbled with the buttons at her throat. "I'm sure you mean well. I need to think it over, Mr. Scottsdale. This is very sudden."

Was that disappointment in his eyes? Hurt? Those eyes probing hers for the truth. Like drawn curtains, Aynsley shuttered her thoughts lest he read them.

"Of course, Miss O'Brien, I understand." He bit off the last word hard. With a curt nod, he stalked toward the house.

As Nolan strode away, she noticed his limp for the first time. Had he been injured in battle? Each footstep fell quicker as though he couldn't put distance between them soon enough. Away from her. Like a swollen creek rippling and surging down from the hills, the cold emptiness of life crashed into her.

Aynsley's trembling knees carried her the remaining distance to the orchard where she sank beneath an apple tree and buried her head in her hands. All the captive tears she had restrained for days squeezed into the open. The trickle quickly gushed into a torrent.

"No, Nolan, you don't understand anything at all."

Nolan swung up on his horse and tightened his knees against Thunder's sides. The horse started into a lope as though sensing his master's mood.

Feeling guilty for starting the older horse off at a quick pace, Nolan murmured, "Sorry, old boy." Once off the grounds of Windy Holler, he pulled the reins and slowed him. Nolan puffed out a long breath. Memories of other days in that long, grassy lane filtered into his thoughts the way sunlight filtered through the clouds. He'd never have thought a day would rise when he'd hurry to get away.

He had been sorely mistaken.

Even after four years, the bitterness hadn't dulled. Rather, it had sharpened. Only to himself did he admit he missed her. Missed everything about her. Worst of all, he missed reading to her. She would sit against a tree, a faraway stare lighting her eyes as the words carried them to a new adventure—a world belonging to them. But Aynsley had silenced the chapter on their story.

His heart squeezed, the familiar throb shaking him every time he thought of her.

I was a fool to think she loved me, and I'm a fool to think she'll marry me.

The wind scraped across Nolan's sunburned neck like sandpaper. The shocked, horrified look on her face when he'd proposed cut deeply. And yet, he would marry her if she decided to have him anyhow.

Nolan glanced heavenward and scanned the blue sky. Last evening, as he prayed, he'd felt sure he was doing the right thing. Where had his peace fled?

Up ahead, a rider on a mule rounded the bend and ambled toward him. The wide-brimmed straw hat cast a shadow over the man's face. As he neared, he raised his hand in greeting and reined in the mule.

"Nolan."

The man was his eighteen-year-old brother. Clad in a homespun shirt and overalls, Daniel warily skimmed Nolan from the top of his head to his feet.

Smiling, Nolan held out his hand. "I haven't seen you since you were knee high to a grasshopper."

"It's been a day or two." Without a flicker of emotion, Daniel gripped Nolan's hand and firmly shook it. "That's a fine horse you have. It's a Morgan, ain't it?"

Nolan nodded. "This is Thunder. He and I have been through thick and thin."

Reaching across, Daniel ran his hand over Thunder's neck

and patted him. "Mother sent me to look for you."

A thrum of hope quickened Nolan's heart. If Mother relented, he could go home and spare Aynsley from making a difficult choice. At least where it concerned him.

Daniel shook his head. "She says don't ever come back."

A dreadful numbness rolled over Nolan like a dark wave. For the first time, a glint of apology cracked Daniel's demeanor. He squirmed under Nolan's stare. "It warn't my idea. The Lord knows I could use help, and it'd be all right to have you around again. But it ain't my farm."

"No need to explain, brother."

"Just so you know, when I get my own farm, you'll be welcome on my doorstep."

"Thank you." Nolan rested a hand on Daniel's shoulder. A hint of affection relaxed the somber features of his younger sibling.

"What are you gonna do?"

"I haven't decided." Nolan rubbed his thumbs against the reins in his palms. "I'm staying at the O'Brien place. In the old cabin."

Daniel's dark eyebrows raised. "Truly?"

"Yes. Miss O'Brien offered to let me stay until I find a place. I might farm Windy Holler."

Whistling long and low, Daniel pushed the brim of his hat up with his forefinger. A bit of a smirk hitched up the corners of his mouth. "If Mother knew, she'd flitter and fall back."

Despite himself, Nolan chuckled. "She would."

"Good for you. I envy you that farmland. It'll make you good crops."

"It's lain fallow for too long. The ground will be hard to stir, but I'm willing to make a go of it, if Miss O'Brien agrees."

"She'd be silly if she didn't. If I thought I'd have half a chance farming it, I'd defy Mother in a heartbeat."

Good thing Daniel didn't realize what was at stake. If he

knew Aynsley was part of the deal, he might try his hand at winning her. "Mother is a formidable woman."

"Yep, but she ain't invincible." Daniel nudged his mule's sides and turned him homeward. "I've never understood her dislike of Miss Aynsley."

"Neither have I."

"Oh, well. At least, Miss Aynsley won't be alone. Eleazar does his best, but he's getting older. I feel better knowin' you're there."

After a final handshake, Daniel headed down the narrow, rutted road while Nolan watched until his brother rounded the bend.

He filled his lungs with the clean Ozark air and exhaled slowly. Sending Daniel with a message wasn't idle bluster.

Mother had drawn a line in the dirt with the barrel of a rifle.

CHAPTER FIVE

Too tense to sit on the sofa, Aynsley paced the oak leaf rug, waiting for Nolan. After supper, she'd sent Eleazar to fetch him. An afternoon of brooding and praying had made up her mind. With quaking fingers, she tugged the stays squeezing her ribcage. Whoever had devised such an invention should be shot.

The sound of thumping boots crossed the porch and entered the breezeway. Coming to a standstill, Aynsley smoothed her skirt and composed her face.

A moment later, Nolan entered. In Uncle's clothes, he looked comical, but laughter had forsaken her. His gaze centered on her, questioning, but he said nothing.

If the floor would simply swallow her. Aynsley thrust her hands together behind her back and steadied her voice, determined not to betray her turmoil. "I've considered the matter, and I'll accept your hand."

A glimmer of pleasure and relief softened the intensity of Nolan's stare. "Thank you."

"You're free to change your mind at any time, though," she hurried on.

"I won't." He moved closer but maintained a respectable distance. "I know you're worried about what's expected of you … as a wife. I trust we can live amicably, workin' together for each other's benefit."

"I agree." Her knees wobbled undetected beneath her skirts.

"Good."

Silence permeated the room while they beheld each other, the years melting away, and for a mere instant, they were simply Aynsley and Nolan. Such a feeling was dangerously intoxicating.

Nolan dragged his gaze to the window. "How soon do you want to wed?"

Aynsley swallowed a dry lump in her throat. "Would the day after tomorrow suit you?"

"It does."

"Very well. Becca and I will have time to make a suit of clothes that will fit you. You must be uncomfortable."

A grin quirked one side of his mouth. "I'm obliged. Thank you." Without looking at her, Nolan stepped toward the door. A second later, the doorknob jangled to no avail. Aynsley chewed the inside of her cheek. The wretched door stuck, as it did betimes.

"It's still cantankerous, I see." Nolan pounded it in the right spot, and the hinges swung open . Of course, he would recall how to do it.

He ducked his broad, six-foot-four frame beneath the doorway, and Aynsley stifled a sigh. How much did Nolan bother to remember?

"Mr. Nolan, I'm right glad to see the clothes fit."

With a final pat on Thunder's neck, Nolan surveyed himself—the navy pants and ivory-colored shirt topped by a navy vest. "It fits fine, Becca. I haven't felt at home in a suit of clothes since leaving."

A delighted smile crinkled the skin around Becca's brown eyes. "It does my heart good to hear it." With a furtive glance around, she stepped closer. "I'd like a word 'fore Miss Aynsley comes."

"Certainly."

"You got to realize somethin' before you wed today. Miss Aynsley has a heart of gold, but she's not 'zactly the way you recollect. Not quite as shy or as gentle. These years have hardened her in places. In other ways, they've strengthened her." Becca peered closely at Nolan. "And I'm sure you're not all the same either."

The sounds of cannon fire and shouts of men rumbled through his thoughts, an unwelcome interruption. "No, not quite." He tightened his jaw.

"What I'm gettin' at is simple, really. Gentle Miss Aynsley in the hardened places, but don't squash her strength. And allow her to do the same for you. The marriage road is long and rocky enough without two people pulling 'gainst each other."

"I appreciate the advice and will pay it heed." Nolan glanced up as Aynsley shut the door and descended the porch steps. "You're a good friend."

"You've nothing to fear as long as you treat Miss Aynsley good." Stepping away, she flashed a grin and a wink.

Despite the nervousness rising, Nolan chuckled. Becca was as good as her word, even in jest. While Aynsley neared, he studied his bride-to-be. A brown gingham bonnet hid most of her thick, raven locks, casting a shadow across her pale face. Her matching, wide-checked gingham dress—the color of chocolate—swathed her petite frame, her waist divulging evidence of lean meals and long hours of tireless work to maintain the farm. A lace collar, probably Aynsley's handiwork, draped around her neck. A pearl brooch nestled at the base of her throat.

She was tiny to the point of frailness, but Becca was right. He sensed strength underneath.

When she reached the buckboard, she settled her turbulent gaze on his. Trepidation pulled her lips together in a tight, narrow line, and guilt kicked him in the gut. He was no better than a thief, stealing her independence.

Without a word of greeting, she held out her hand, waiting for his assistance. He closed his fingers around hers and noticed her shabby gloves. Aynsley climbed into the buckboard and released his hand as soon as she gained her footing.

Nolan waited until she was settled on the seat. When she folded her hands into her lap, he cleared his throat. "Miss O'Brien."

She glanced up.

"All I wish is to protect you and restore your beloved home. Together, I believe you and I will accomplish it, Lord willing. Don't be distressed."

Tugging a handkerchief from her sleeve, Aynsley wound it through her fingers. Immediately, Nolan recognized the violet flourish as he glimpsed an embroidered *S* in one corner. "Carrying your mother's handkerchief on this special day?"

"You remember it?"

"Certainly." How could he forget? After all, it was her prized possession, a special memento of her mother. When Aynsley was a child, she often carried it everywhere. "I think your mother would be pleased."

"I hope so."

The doubt in her voice jabbed him. Nolan rubbed his jaw. "We don't have to do this."

"We have no choice."

"There's always a choice. You're not trapped."

Aynsley raised her eyebrows, tipping her head sideways. "I'm not? Tell me how."

How could he do this to her? If marrying him was abhorrent to her, he couldn't do it, no matter the cost. He shifted from the buckboard, shaking his head. "I can't do this to you. Perhaps there's someone else who might be willing."

"No, there's no one else. Nolan, wait." She slammed her eyes shut as if his name had accidentally slipped out.

He waited, a knot clenching his stomach.

Aynsley curled her fingers around the armrest. "I'm sorry for the way that sounded. You're not trapping me, but the trouble goes deeper. You're choosing to bind yourself in marriage. Losing the land is the worst that can happen to me."

"I daresay it isn't," Nolan murmured low. "You're in a vulnerable position."

Scarlet flooded her cheeks. "I can handle myself and a gun, but you're missing my point. You've much more to lose. What if, in a few years, you regret it? You're giving up every opportunity ahead of you. Don't relinquish your freedom for me."

She was afraid he would regret it? If only she knew. "I know exactly what I'm doing."

"Do you?"

"More than you realize." Maybe humor would help. "Do you need me to ask your hand in marriage again? How 'bout I get down on one knee?"

The crimson in her cheeks flamed into her forehead as she twisted the handkerchief harder. "No."

"I want to be a good provider. Our union, I expect, will be one of friendship."

"Married couples have to be friends?" Aynsley eyes snapped up, a hard glint darkening those brown depths with thoughts he couldn't decipher.

Heavens above. He'd stepped on a nerve somehow. Grimacing, Nolan tugged his collar. *Answer careful, man.* "It's better than being strangers."

"And are we strangers, Mr. Scottsdale?"

Her emphasis on his last name chipped like a pickaxe on stone. "When you address me like that, we are."

"Ah. But you call me Miss O'Brien."

"Then I suggest we quit tossing our last names at each other's heads and call one another by our given names."

A hint of triumph curved Aynsley's lips. "You admit to bandying my name at me?"

"Do you admit to doing the same?" Nolan quirked an eyebrow.

"Never." Her gaze collapsed to the handkerchief clutched in her hands.

With a pang, Nolan remembered Becca's gentle advice. Gone was the shy, gentle girl he'd dearly loved. Yet, no matter how she had changed, he wanted nothing more than to live by her side. What would she say if he dared tell her? He rested his hand over her clenched ones.

"Aynsley, will you marry me?"

She pulled her bottom lip between her teeth with a shuddering breath while he waited, his pulse pounding in his neck. He sensed her grappling for control.

Finally, she lifted her head. "If you're certain, then I will."

Relief surged as he clasped her hands lightly before releasing them. While he rounded the buckboard, Aynsley studied his face. "If you live to regret it, don't blame me."

Holding onto her stare, Nolan stepped into the rig and grabbed the reins. "I never shall."

CHAPTER SIX

The buckboard jostled over smooth stones as Thunder pulled it through the shallow creek. The water splashed against the spokes of the wheels and swirled around the horse's ankles. A fresh, cool breeze nipped along the water and doused the edges of Aynsley's worries.

Retying her bonnet more firmly under her chin, she winced, recalling her words and attitude. Poor Nolan didn't realize the price of his commitment. A weak-minded wife. Damaged.

He never knew the real reason Uncle Stewart hadn't sent her to school. Certainly, he'd paid a teacher to help her, but Aynsley struggled. The words and letters made no sense.

Shame soured Aynsley's stomach, and she pressed her hand against its roiling. At night, she'd heard Uncle Stewart and Aunt Eva's worries. How could a young girl, seemingly normal, have the inability to read and comprehend the meaning? And Elnora had never failed to recount Aynsley's shortcomings in the privacy of their room.

Her condition colored her entire life. Every day, a heavy curtain blockaded her advancement to simply being normal.

Recipes and letters broke her out into a cold sweat. Bible readings terrorized her, though she always managed to excuse her way out of it. Books and their lovely worlds barred her from knowledge and wonderful, unseen places she would never visit.

When Nolan used to read to her, the curtain had been drawn aside. Listening to the rise and fall of his intonations, she had glimpsed the world beyond the Ozarks.

If she were so weak-minded, how could she understand spoken words?

Yet she must be. No matter how hard she tried, written words evaded her grasp. Words were words, whether written or spoken. Tilting her head, she peeped around the side of her bonnet at Nolan. Helplessness tightened her throat.

Through her uncle and aunt's guidance, she'd learned to carry herself as a lady, speak as though she were educated, and hide her secret.

She was a fraud, and her future husband had no idea.

Sunbeams highlighted Nolan's placid features and flecked gold through his sandy hair. Harsh, unforgiving times in a cavalry saddle had etched premature lines across his forehead, belying his twenty-four years. When he glanced at her, time dissolved like wax under a flame.

His blue eyes flickered as if he'd caught her. "What are you thinking about?"

Steadying her breath, Aynsley focused on a squirrel scurrying up a tree. "That's for me to know."

"Not yet married and already keeping secrets from me."

She suppressed a shudder. "A woman is entitled to a few. I expect you have some too."

"Mayhap." Nolan straightened. "Someone's coming up the road."

Three men ambled toward them on horses, their sidearms glinting in their holsters. A homemade sling bound one of the men's arms. Though hats darkened their faces, Aynsley recognized them. Her insides withered. "It's Zeke Hoskin and his brothers. Are you armed?"

"Always."

His quiet, assured manner eased her apprehension very little. The Hoskins meant trouble, and they aimed it at her. Nolan slowed their horse as the men approached. Thick and brawny, the brothers dwarfed most men in the county. All except Nolan, who bested them by a few inches.

The oldest, Zeke, held up a hand. "Nolan Scottsdale, be that you?"

"It is." Nolan stopped the buckboard.

"Too bad a Reb bullet didn't knock you from the saddle."

Unruffled, Nolan offered a smile. "It did, but the Good Lord had other plans."

Grunting, Zeke stroked the russet beard draped over his chest. "I wonder. My business ain't with you but with this gal."

"Miss Aynsley and I are on our way to be married."

The men hooted, their guffaws an ugly clatter through the trees. "Boys, this Yankee is gonna have a hard time tamin' that little Reb." Zeke slapped his thigh.

"I'd pay good money to see it." Ardy crossed his muscled arms, his grin sporting a missing front tooth.

Nolan scooted forward as if to rise, but Aynsley gripped a restraining hand on his forearm. She raised her chin. "All right. You've had your joke, Mr. Hoskin. Let's get down to business."

The laughter dried up as the men's faces hardened. Zeke pointed a gritty finger. "You know what we want. Your uncle died a foolish man, and we ain't about to forget the bullet you put in Tom's arm." He gestured to his wounded brother.

"My aim will be better next time."

Tom spit a stream of tobacco juice at Thunder's hooves. "So will mine."

Hiding the fear icing her veins, Aynsley scooted forward on the seat, an angry scowl plastered on her face. "I'm not as patient as Uncle Stewart. Keep out of Windy Holler."

"We're not patient either, but I'd rather not see a woman's blood spilt. You'd best tend to business, and we'll forget Tom's ailment."

Like a lightning flash, the barrel of a pistol aimed straight at Zeke Hoskin's heart. The hammer cocked under Nolan's thumb. The three men froze as he angled his body in front of Aynsley's.

"That's enough. No more threatening my bride. You're dealing with me."

For a long minute, a few screeching blue jays filled the silence. Aynsley's heart stampeded against her ribs as she resisted the urge to lean against the protective cover of Nolan's back.

Crimson anger flushed upward from Zeke's beard. "You don't know who you're messing with, but that gal had better tell you real quick, or you'll both be joinin' her uncle when you least expect it."

"I know you, and I'll be watching."

"You do that." Zeke jerked his head toward his brothers. "We'll be moving along, but we're not done."

One by one, they kicked their horses' sides and trotted down the road, the dust rising from their trail. Swiveling to watch their hasty retreat, Nolan eased the hammer into its place.

Expelling a pent-up breath, Aynsley slumped against the seat, unable to control her quivering limbs. Unwanted scenes flooded her mind.

Nolan tucked the pistol into his jacket and tapped the reins across Thunder. Aynsley swayed with the buckboard's motion, wishing the earth to swallow her up.

Relaxing against the seat, Nolan eyed Aynsley as if seeing

her for the first time and cleared his throat. "I reckon I'm behind. Suppose you catch me up. Did they kill your uncle?" The words exploded inside Aynsley like the gaping wound in Uncle Stewart's chest. Her eyes slammed shut against the memory.

"Aynsley, did they?"

Unable to utter the answer, she nodded.

"And they are roaming free?"

"There's no law nowadays. The Hoskins are the law in this county, and no one will stand up to them. It's not a clear case of murder. They claim self-defense."

The skin between Nolan's brows pinched together. "And you shot Tom?" His frown deepened in disbelief.

"I did, and I hit exactly where I intended. They came to Windy Holler, threatening Uncle Stewart. The argument got heated, especially when Uncle wouldn't listen." She closed her fingers around her knees, bracing herself against the inner turmoil. "I was holding the rifle at the parlor window. I'd opened it and taken aim in case things went amiss. And they did. Eleazar was positioned at the barn. When Uncle drew his pistol, Tom shot him … in the chest."

She clenched her jaw against the grief surging up her throat while Nolan waited in silence. Steadying the waver in her voice, she continued. "I shot Tom, and Eleazar fired from the barn. He shot Zeke's hat off his head. It wouldn't do for him to kill a white man."

"They'd lynch him, for sure."

"The Hoskins left, but not before they torched the barn. I ran to Uncle Stewart, but there was nothing I could do."

Nolan leaned closer. "You haven't told me why."

Nearby, a robin rooted in the dirt, and Aynsley wondered how the world dared be beautiful in the midst of such ugliness. "They wanted him to kick Eleazar and Becca off the place, drive them out of the county. They're both free, and

Windy Holler is their home too. Now, they're after me to do it. I will not."

"Why haven't you already told me?"

Though his tone held no censure, she snapped her head toward him. "First, I find myself sole heir, then you show up on my doorstep after four years and promptly ask to marry me the next day. I didn't want to tell you the extent of my situation because I know you. You're an honorable man. I didn't want to take advantage of it."

"You were giving me room to have second thoughts?"

"Yes."

"It wouldn't have made a difference. Once I set my mind to something, there's no changing."

Aynsley cringed. "I might have to remind you of that someday. You don't realize what you've taken on."

"With God's help, we'll manage." His eyes watchful, Nolan scanned the hills. "We'd better come home another way."

Aynsley's stomach plummeted. When would every shadow, tree, hill, or stone cease to be a potential threat? "There's no getting away from the Hoskins. May the Lord forgive me, but I almost wish I'd killed Tom."

She recalled the cold resolve in his granite eyes while he'd stared a hole through her. Her fingertips grazed the muff pistol nestled inside her pocket, but it did little to bolster her courage.

Tom Hoskin would make her pay.

CHAPTER SEVEN

"Miss Aynsley doesn't care for public displays of affection, so we'll forgo the kiss," Nolan informed the Justice of the Peace before they exchanged vows.

Aynsley rewarded him with a ghost of a smile and looked down at her feet. A twinge of disappointment goaded Nolan, but he hid it while Mr. Scarbrough pulled a black book from his desk and stood.

"Very well. Can't say I blame the lady. There's a time and place for such things." Mr. Scarbrough straightened the spectacles on his nose and thumbed through the yellowed, crackling pages.

Rolling his shoulders to relieve the taut muscles, Nolan pulled in a breath. Would a day come when there was a time and place in Aynsley's heart for him?

"Are you young folks ready? You both look a mite pale."

They nodded mutely. A hint of amusement shimmied across Mr. Scarbrough's mouth. "Very well. Let us ask the Lord's blessing over this union."

In the dim, musty cabin, the simple prayer floated upward

and permeated the air, a sweet stillness like the offering of incense.

Nolan mouthed his own prayer, a silent petition that God alone heard. Would he be able to protect Aynsley? Could he shield Eleazar and Becca from harm? The last thing they needed was to dig his grave next to Stewart O'Brien's. He couldn't count on his family to come to their aid.

You, Father, are the only One Who can help us.

"Will you take Miss O'Brien's hand in yours?"

Raising his head, Nolan outstretched his palm toward Aynsley. After a slight hesitation, she peeped up at him and gingerly settled her fingertips into his palm. He enclosed her hand within a firm grip and squeezed.

Her solemn face remained impassive, her thoughts veiled from him.

But not forever, Aynsley.

Sunlight sifted through the dust hovering in the small room while they repeated their vows to each other. His bride anchored her unwavering gaze on the top button of his shirt. With each word, her wan face grew paler. Nolan's heart panged.

And to think he'd once believed she loved him.

"I now pronounce you man and wife." Mr. Scarbrough closed the book and nodded toward the table. "We'll sign the license, and then you can be on your way."

Flinching, Aynsley slipped her hand from Nolan's. "Sign?"

"Yes, ma'am." Mr. Scarbrough rounded the table.

"Do I sign my maiden name or my ... new one?"

"Your maiden name."

Visible relief passed over Aynsley's face as she approached and took the pen Mr. Scarbrough held out. Bending over the paper, she poised the pen between her fingers.

"Sign here." The Justice of the Peace tapped the spot.

"Of course." Aynsley closed her eyes and paused as though settling herself.

Startled, Nolan touched her shoulder. "Do you feel ill?"

Her eyes flew open. Blinking, she shook her head. "I'm all right." Nervousness edged her voice. Once more, Aynsley closed her eyes then signed her name with quick, deft strokes. Seeming relieved, she straightened and offered him the pen.

After Nolan signed his name and paid Mr. Scarbrough, he offered Aynsley his arm. Her gloved fingers trembled on his sleeve as they stepped into the fresh air.

Next came Mr. Kirby's office. After exchanging greetings and congratulations, the lawyer readied the papers for Aynsley's signature. Again, she closed her eyes while signing her name. Surely, she wouldn't faint.

With the papers in tow, they exited the building, and Nolan pulled Aynsley closer.

"Becca packed dinner for us. She put it under the seat. Would you like to stop somewhere along the way home and eat?" He gripped her elbow as she climbed into the buckboard.

Averting her gaze, Aynsley settled herself, smoothing her skirts. "If you would like to."

How he wished he could reach the inward girl he knew. She was there, somewhere. Finding her was another matter. As he popped the reins, he remembered a place deep in the woods yet not far from Windy Holler.

Mindful of the Hoskins, Nolan drove another way home. The miles rolled under the rig's wheels, carrying them over creeks and grassy lanes, past small farmhouses and cabins. Slowing Thunder's pace, Nolan guided him behind a stand of several oaks.

Aynsley looked around. "What are we doing?"

"Eating dinner." After swinging to the ground, Nolan pulled the basket from beneath the seat while Aynsley draped the quilt over her arm and climbed down. "Follow me, Mrs. Scottsdale."

Aynsley's pale face bloomed the loveliest shade of rose, and his satisfaction threatened to bubble into a chortle. Nolan held his lips steady, however. Wouldn't do to get her dander up.

The brush of her skirts against the grass told him that she followed closely over sparse rocks while they wound through the woods. Her pace quickened.

"I remember this path, except we used to come through Uncle Stewart's field." Wonder filled her words.

"The very one." Nolan shifted the weight of the basket into his other hand. They walked the rest of the way in silence until they emerged into a clearing.

Stopping alongside him, Aynsley raised her head and took a long breath. Like a green ribbon threaded with silver, the creek sparkled in the sunshine. Wildflowers swayed among the tall grass, the colors speckling the green canvas untouched by human hands.

Aynsley plucked a purple flower and brought it to her nose. "After all your travels, I'm surprised you remember this place."

"I could never forget it." *Or you.*

She seemed to ponder his words. After moving to a patch of shade, she spread the quilt and sat. With a deft tug, she freed her head of the bonnet. Her keen gaze roved the clearing. "It's like another world."

Like sentinels, the woods bordered the field on all sides. Nolan set the basket between them and knelt. "And yet it's caught in the middle."

"Right smack dab in it."

"A lot of times, the night before going into battle, I thought of this place, of our good times here."

Aynsley studied him. "You mentioned being wounded to Zeke." Concern filled her eyes. "I noticed your limp."

Rather than squirm, Nolan stretched out his legs instead. "I don't speak of it unless I have to. It happened early in the war."

"Where?"

"Antietam."

Shuddering, Aynsley rubbed her arms. "I'm sorry."

"No need. I'm blessed to be alive. To complain about my limp would be a sin against those who suffered far worse."

The basket crackled as Aynsley opened it. With his assistance, she fixed the plates. "Becca must've wanted our wedding dinner to be special. Fried chicken, purple hull peas, biscuits, gravy, and cake. She must have a stash of sugar somewhere." A grin curved her lips. "Bless her."

"She's one of a kind, though I'll never fully forgive her for busting my britches when I was nine."

"You stole her apple pie."

"She never found the evidence."

"I wonder why." Arching her eyebrows, Aynsley patted her stomach. Nolan laughed without a speck of shame.

Silence descended as they watched each other, their unspoken thoughts whispering between them. After taking a bite of chicken, Aynsley dabbed her mouth with the handkerchief.

Nolan swallowed a forkful of purple hull peas. "How old were you when your uncle gave you that handkerchief?"

"I think I was five." She spread it out on her palm and thoughtfully traced the embroidered *S* in one corner, working her way around the violet pansies—each bloom stitched in the other corners. "I feel a bit guilty keeping it."

"What do you mean?"

"My mother made a matching set—one for Uncle Stewart and one for her. This one was hers. When she died, Uncle

Stewart kept it. He put his in Mother's hands to be buried with her. I should've buried this one with him, but I couldn't bring myself to do it."

How Nolan yearned to nestle Aynsley against his chest and comfort her. "I'm certain your uncle and mother would want you to keep it."

"I keep telling myself this."

"It's true."

"Perhaps." She folded it across her lap. "She made them when she was eight years old. Uncle Stewart told me that Mother embroidered red pansies on his because it meant love and affection. And his S was red instead of violet. I've often imagined what it looked like."

"Your mother must've been a talented seamstress."

"So I've been told." Aynsley nibbled a biscuit, her brow crinkled in thought. "Do you think we'll survive this?"

"The Lord above knows. All we can do is depend on Him to get us through."

"The Hoskins won't stop."

"Uncertainty will be a part of our lives for a long time, maybe all of it. But I can promise you, Aynsley, I'll never leave your side as long as the Lord wills it."

Aynsley's chin tremored, but her lips remained still.

CHAPTER EIGHT

"She's here. Elnora's here." Clutching her skirts in her fists, Becca jogged toward them as Nolan helped Aynsley from the buckboard.

"Already?" Aynsley reeled against Nolan but quickly straightened. His hand closed around her elbow while she gathered composure.

"She's spoutin' orders and taking up residence in Mr. and Mrs. O'Brien's room," Becca hissed. "Like she owns the place."

Indignation kindled in Aynsley's veins. She would have to take things in hand, or her cousin would make everyone's life miserable. Then she remembered Nolan. Their marriage.

Aynsley glanced at him. "I'll get her out of Uncle and Aunt's room. We stay there."

Nolan's stare traveled to the upstairs window on the north side of the dogtrot. "I don't want to cause any hardship."

"Nonsense. You need to be near when the Hoskins show up."

"You're right." A grim line tightened his lips. "I'll get my things."

Before either of them moved, a door opened, and a tall

woman glided into the dogtrot. She whisked across the porch and paused. "Aynsley."

"Elnora." She forced her leaden feet to move. "I wasn't expecting you so soon."

"Since Albert died, there's nothing holding me at Vicksburg. With Papa's untimely passing, it seemed right to come home."

Dread curdled Aynsley's stomach. "What do you mean?"

"I'm here. To stay." A triumphant smile, devoid of warmth, curled Elnora's lips. Her cool green eyes breezed over Aynsley from head to foot.

A muffled groan seeped from Becca as she headed toward the back of the house. "Lord, help us."

Indeed. Hating the way Elnora towered over her, especially from the porch, Aynsley clipped up the steps. "We need to talk privately. You may change your mind once we've discussed things."

"Such as what?" Elnora's flinty stare burned into hers. Then her eyes rounded as she gaped over Aynsley's shoulder. "Nolan Scottsdale."

"It's been a long time." Nolan tipped his head, his eyes wary.

"What are you doing here?"

"I'm Aynsley's husband," he said, his tone hinting pride.

The color fled Elnora's face. "That can't be. When did this happen?"

"Today." A sunny smile spread across Nolan's face as though he were the happiest man in the world.

"You certainly didn't waste any time and Papa not even cold in the ground."

Nolan's expression evaporated like a morning mist. "That'll do, Elnora."

His strength bolstered Aynsley's. Of all people, he

understood her cousin's ways. Elnora drew an indignant breath.

Before she could retort, a shaded movement caught Aynsley's eyes.

"Mama?"

With a distracted wave, Elnora gestured for the girl to come. Not more than four, she was a lovely miniature of Elnora from her cornsilk curls to her rosebud lips. She tottered across the space and threw herself against her mother.

"You've not met Zadie Charlotte. Zadie, this is your cousin Aynsley."

Smiling, Aynsley extended her hand. "Hello. I'm glad to meet you at last."

Genuine terror shimmered in Zadie's eyes. Clutching fistfuls of Elnora's skirts, she buried her face in them. "No," she shrieked. "Mama, help!"

"It's all right, darlin'." Elnora's arm rounded the child's shoulders. "She won't hurt you."

Horrified, Aynsley snatched away her hand. "What do you mean?"

Ignoring her, Elnora led the whimpering girl inside and slammed the parlor door in Aynsley's face.

Helplessness crowded Aynsley, drowning out every sight and sound. "How can I bear this, Lord?" she murmured.

A sturdy hand closed over her shoulder. Aynsley gasped, unaware that Nolan had been standing behind her. His warm fingers tightened. "You're not going to bear it alone."

Aynsley blinked hot tears. "Are you still so sure? It's not too late to run."

"On the contrary, battle suits me." Nolan slid her a wink. Despite herself, Aynsley choked out a small laugh and dabbed the handkerchief against her nose.

With a satisfied nod, he released her and hopped off the porch.

While she watched, all the love she'd ever felt for him dizzied her senses. Nolan was her husband. Her impossible dream had somehow become reality.

But would it last?

"Papa willed Windy Holler to you?" Elnora spat, springing from the rocking chair. "I don't believe it."

"I couldn't either," Aynsley faltered. "I'm sorry."

"I bet you are." Elnora paced in front of the fireplace, her fingers curled into fists. "I'm his flesh and blood. His daughter."

"You have a home in Vicksburg. Albert provided well for you. I'm sure that's the reason for Uncle Stewart's decision."

Elnora's feet halted, and she crossed her arms. "We lost everything when the Yankees nearly starved us out."

"That was two years ago."

"Believe me, I can count." She tromped to the window and peered across the nighttime landscape. "Then Albert succumbed to the fever a month ago. Papa should've known I needed this place."

"Uncle Stewart didn't realize you were penniless."

"I was getting ready to come when I received word of his … death." She gripped the windowsill.

Pushing away from the mantle, Nolan went to stand behind Aynsley's chair. "Eleazar and I can fix up the cottage for you and Zadie—"

"I'm not about to stay in that dilapidated shack. This is my home, not yours." She arced her hand through the air, the gesture encompassing the room. "I demand to see the will. Now."

"Very well." Nolan pulled the papers from the inner pocket of his waistcoat, his face flushed. He placed them in her outstretched hand.

A tremor snaked down Aynsley's spine as Elnora read them. Surprise fractured the hardened scowl on her face.

"Papa's terms are unusual, to say the least." Elnora narrowed her eyes at Nolan. "No wonder you married Aynsley."

"It's none of your business why I married her."

"That's what you think."

Nolan tugged the papers from Elnora and folded them. "If you wish to remain here, we'll have no trouble from you. Out of respect for your father, we'd like to help, but it's your choice. Don't make it impossible."

Elnora's green eyes frosted. Stiffening, she marched past him and ignored Aynsley altogether. Her skirts whisked through the dogtrot and upstairs to the bedroom where Zadie slept in their childhood bedroom.

Nolan stuffed the papers into his pocket. "I reckon it's good I was taught better than to hit a woman."

"It's hard to do battle without fists."

"There are other ways." His jaw clenched.

Weariness sagged Aynsley, her limbs aching for the comfort of her bed. *The bed.* She sprang from the chair, remembering their situation.

"Nolan, what are we going to do about ..."

He raised his brows. "What is it?"

"Our sleeping arrangements."

"I'd forgotten." Nolan coughed into his hand. "What do you suggest?"

"We have no choice but to share Uncle and Aunt's room."

A tender look smoothed the stern lines around his eyes. "Nothing needs to change between us. I've spent years sleeping anywhere, rarely in a bed. I can make a place on the floor."

"It isn't right. I feel horrible knowing how uncomfortable you'll be."

He waved her comment aside with a reassuring smile. "I'll make do. Why don't you go upstairs and get ready for sleep. I'll come up later."

Unsure whether to feel ashamed or grateful, Aynsley dipped her head. "Thank you." Fixing her gaze on the floor, she padded out of the room.

Awhile later, after she had settled under the quilt, the doorknob twisted and creaked. As Nolan entered then latched the door, Aynsley yanked the cover over her head.

She heard him set the kerosene lamp on the oak chest of drawers. At the foot of the bed, the shuffling of covers reached her ears. He was obviously making a pallet. Again, guilt pricked her. To sleep on a hard floor after years away from home and mere inches from a bed was cruel. And on his wedding night.

The unfastening of his belt came next. With a thump, Nolan's britches hit the floor. She heard them scrape the planks as he picked them up and draped them over the foot of the bed. More shuffling. He plopped a few other things beside the britches. More than likely his waistcoat and shirt.

Aynsley's face burned. The stuffy air under the covers constricted her lungs, making it hard to breathe.

"You can come out for air. I'm decent."

"Well, I never," she sputtered.

"It's threadbare, but I have one nightshirt to my name." Humor edged Nolan's voice. "We may as well get used to each other."

Aynsley pushed the quilt down over her nose and peeped

out. Standing at the foot of the bed, Nolan chuckled and held out his arms, the baggy sleeves dangling at his wrists. "See?"

Relieved, she filled her lungs.

Lowering his arms, Nolan sobered. "It was easier when we were children."

Aynsley feigned ignorance. "What do you mean?"

"Children aren't afraid to be honest. Grown folks hide more. Guess it comes with things life throws at us."

Remaining silent, Aynsley's guilt plunged deeper. When was she completely and honestly herself? Free? Beneath everything, the dread of Nolan learning the truth dogged her. Hunted her down in every moment of happiness. Barricaded her from him.

And yet, there he stood. He planted his hands on the iron bedstead and leaned forward, his blue eyes searching hers. "Who are you, Aynsley?"

Her voice came out in a whisper. "You know who I am."

"We used to understand each other better than anyone else. Can it be that way again?"

"I … I'm not sure."

A rueful smile tugged his lips. "If the Lord allows, we've got a lifetime to figure it out."

Time stretched like a winding trail through the hills. Peaks and valleys. Hidden places obscured from outsiders. A lifetime was too long to hide from herself and him. Old habits and training couldn't be undone in a night, however.

Aynsley fingered a striped, square patch on the quilt. "I'm sorry you're stuck with me."

Sighing, Nolan tunneled his fingers through his sandy hair. "I should be saying the same to you, but I've got a confession."

"What is it?"

Remaining quiet, he waited until she peeked through her

eyelashes. His direct, undaunted stare snagged hers. "I'm not sorry."

Aynsley's pulse thrummed over her temples, thundering like a waterfall, a feeling both exhilarating and terrifying. "Why?"

"Too many reasons to explain, but honesty between us has got to start somewhere. No matter what it is."

He didn't realize what he was saying.

Suddenly chilled on a warm night, Aynsley slinked farther beneath the cover. "All I can do is try, Nolan."

"Rest assured, I'll hold you to it." He stepped onto his makeshift bed of quilts and knelt. "Good night, Mrs. Scottsdale."

The pillow cushioned her head as she sank into it. His assurance gave Aynsley no rest, regardless of the fatigue enveloping her.

CHAPTER NINE

"I'd break enough ground this year to feed the family. It'll be easier to watch over. Maybe plant a small patch of cotton for market." Eleazar rechecked the mule's harness while Nolan readied the plow.

"I agree." Straightening, he looked across the east field. The fallow ground stretched in front of him, the spring grass already taking hold. "I noticed the garden you've started behind the house."

"Best to be prepared in case the crops get ruined." Eleazar swiped a kerchief across the beads of sweat already speckling his forehead. He tilted his hat to deflect the sun's rising rays. "A garden is easier to defend. Folks may say the war is over, but they don't act like it."

"It's hard to step out of a rut, and we've dug a deep one."

"If we don't, we're gonna trip flat on our faces."

"Then we'd better help each other out." Stepping behind the plow, Nolan lifted the straps over his shoulders and gripped the handles.

"Most folks don't want that kind of help. It takes the Lord's hand." Eleazar stuffed the kerchief into the pocket of his overalls. "I'm mighty glad you're here, Mr. Nolan. It'll be easier with two of us watchin' and workin' the place."

"I owe you a debt I can't pay. I'm thankful you stayed with Aynsley."

"We couldn't leave her alone." Glancing toward the house, Eleazar watched Becca casting feed to the chickens. "I don't want to leave. Windy Holler is my home too, but if the Hoskins don't stop, we'll have to go. For all our sakes."

"Let's not cross any bridges unless we're forced. I've learned to take things one day at a time. It's all we've got."

"True enough. I'd better get started. It's a mercy we saved these plows from the barn." Eleazar stepped over to his waiting mule and began hitching up another plow.

At Nolan's command, the mule stepped forward, and the plow bit into the earth, turning over the dirt. The vibrations hummed along the handles and up Nolan's arms as he guided the animal. Step after step, the new row grew longer and straight.

The work was honest, hot, unforgiving, and nothing like he'd ever planned for his future. Though he'd grown up behind a plow, his heart had been set on doctoring. In school, he had devoted himself to his studies, dreaming of the day he would tend the hurts and ailments of people.

The sun climbed higher, and the handles bit into the calluses of his palms. After half a dozen rows, Nolan paused to rip his kerchief and wrap them. Tonight, the blisters would throb, but his hands would get tougher. With the pain, he'd have no time to think of unfulfilled dreams or screams on the battlefield.

Raising his eyes, he spied Aynsley picking her way across the rows, carrying a water pail. He mopped a gritty sleeve across his forehead and waited. Her tiny boots mashed through the clods. The simple, gray work dress swathed her petite frame, a bit too thin from scant meals.

He'd change that with the Lord's help.

When she tilted up her head, the sunlight banished the shadows that the bonnet cast over her face. His heart soared. For her, he would plow a thousand fields, no matter his dreams of doctoring.

Unaware of his thoughts, Aynsley stepped alongside him. "I brought water. You must be thirsty."

"I am." Upturning the dipper, Nolan drained it, the cold well water dousing his parched tongue and throat. "The best refreshment in all the world. Thank you."

Nodding, Aynsley smiled as he drank another dipperful. He smacked his lips. "How are things at the house?"

"About as you'd expect. Elnora is sulking, refusing to lift a finger to help."

"I'll put a stop to that. Everyone has to pull their weight here." Nolan removed his hat and fanned his face.

"She's delicate." Aynsley said it as if tasting something sour.

"Not hardly. She's tough as hardtack."

Aynsley's shoulders dipped with her wistful sigh. "But she's as beautiful as ever."

What a thing to say. "Whatever you do, never envy Elnora." His eyes wandered over her face. "Would you believe me if I said you're much more beautiful?"

Startled, she batted her eyelashes and shook her head. "No. I'm like a mouse. Tiny. Drab gray."

"Whatever you are, Mrs. Scottsdale, you're not a mouse, nor are you drab." Nolan stopped himself before he said too much.

"I need to get this to Eleazar." Looking down at her feet, she scurried onward across the field.

How can I reach you?

While he popped the straps across the mule, Nolan remembered her panicked eyes peeking at him over the edge of the quilt. In that instant, everything in him yearned to win Aynsley's trust and eventually her love.

Until then, being married would have to be enough until they could share their lives. Or would they simply retain a shadow of their old comradery?

Nolan trekked through the dirt clods while the mule pulled the plow, the fresh soil clumping against his boots. His thoughts plowed in rhythm with his steps, preparing a way to reach Aynsley.

He remembered their times in the orchard when he read stories. How she loved listening to them.

Aynsley's laugh trickled into his thoughts. Across the way, she and Eleazar talked together, their conversation rippling across the wind. Loneliness tugged at him, and he clutched the plow handles harder. He'd faced enough of it during the past four years. Time to get reacquainted with living.

Looking ahead, Nolan focused on the tree line at the edge of the field and cleared his rambling mind. Crooked rows wouldn't do any of them good.

Concentrating on the furrows in front of her, Aynsley stepped across each one, careful not to trip. The water pail's handle bit into her palm. She switched it to her other hand just as her boot caught on a large clod. She staggered a few steps but remained upright.

Though Nolan was farther down the field, she felt his watchful eyes. Her face burned. Keeping her head lowered, she trudged onward until she entered the yard. Drawing a relieved breath, she headed for the breezeway.

Zadie's cheerful chatter met Aynsley's ears as she climbed the steps. The little girl sprawled at Elnora's feet, rolling onto her back while brandishing a stick.

"Careful, darlin', you might hit Mama," Elnora cautioned, shifting in the rocking chair. Zadie giggled and waved the stick closer to Elnora's legs. Glancing up, she spied Aynsley. Her eyes widened.

Dropping the stick, Zadie scrambled to her feet. "NO!" With a screech, she dashed through the breezeway and hopped down the steps. She careened into Becca who was returning from the garden.

"Woah, child. You 'bout run me over." Becca shifted the basket of vegetables onto her hip.

"Help me." Zadie flapped her hands, and Becca scooped up the child with an arm, her wise glance meeting Aynsley's horrified one.

Becca shushed the whimpering child. "Ain't nothin' gonna hurt you, Zadie Charlotte. We all love you. Come on with Aunt Becca, and we'll wash these vegetables together."

She climbed the steps and headed toward the kitchen. As they neared Aynsley, Zadie hid her face against Becca's shoulder.

After the kitchen door swung shut, Aynsley hung the water pail on a peg and faced Elnora.

"Why is Zadie frightened of me? What have you told her?"

Elnora shrugged. "You should know."

"Well, I don't."

"I told her the truth."

Aynsley crossed her arms. "And what *truth* is that?"

With a hooded glance, Elnora ran a thumbnail over the armrest. "Your mind. What else? You're not quite like the rest of us. A bit weak-minded and temperamental. Unstable."

Squeezing her eyelids shut, Aynsley strove to keep her voice even. "The only time I'm *unstable* is when you mention it."

"Anyone who opens a book and sees words scrambling together or dancing around on the page is not *all there*."

Aynsley drew in a deep breath and counted. She mustn't lose control. "I can do anything else. Did you bother telling Zadie that? You've made me out to be some sort of horrible creature. I'm not unstable." Shame coursed through her veins.

"Don't you remember the time you boxed my ears?"

Mortification coiled up within her chest at the memory. Aynsley had been twelve. Uncle had been working hard to teach her to read all that morning, to no avail. She could still hear the rain outside pelting the windows, each one drumming out her concentration. The words had swum, dizzying her senses.

And Elnora had laughed. Not once but with every word Aynsley missed. After Uncle had scolded her, Elnora choked down her giggles, which made it worse.

Aynsley had stuttered over another word, and Elnora laughed so hard that she doubled over. What came next took everyone by surprise, including Aynsley.

Springing from her seat, she had thrown the book onto the floor and lunged at Elnora. Afterward, Uncle spanked Aynsley for her first and only time.

She never attempted to read again.

Banishing the memory from the present, Aynsley opened her eyes and uncrossed her arms. "I apologized again and again, but you won't let me forget it. Did you tell Zadie?"

Elnora's pointed silence was her answer.

"Why would you tell a child something so terrible?"

"She needs to beware of you. You'd better never touch her."

"I … I wouldn't think of it." Pressing a fist against her stomach, Aynsley staggered toward the front porch.

Elnora pushed herself up and followed, her shoes thumping across the floor. "And what about Nolan? Have you told him about your mental deformity?"

"It's none of your business." Aynsley gritted her teeth. "You tend to Zadie and leave us be."

Elnora smirked, triumph flashing in her cool green eyes. "You haven't told. You'd best do it before your children come."

Aynsley bit down a cry, her hand shooting out toward Elnora's cheek before halting in mid-air. Their glares mingled like fire and oil.

Elnora raised her brows. "You see? I'm right."

Waves of nausea rolled over Aynsley. What had she almost done? She lowered her hand and bounded down the steps, away from the very one she'd once loved as a sister. It took everything not to hate her.

Yes, Elnora was right but not about everything.

There would never be any children for her and Nolan.

CHAPTER TEN

"Aynsley, are you going to simply sit there and let your Yankee husband deny me food?" Elnora shoved away the saucer of cornbread.

Nolan worked his jaw and shook his head at Aynsley, his eyes telegraphing her not to answer. "Everyone here pulls their weight, Elnora. That's the way we're going to survive."

"Is that a fact? Remember I lived in Vicksburg through the war. I know about going hungry."

"And I don't intend for that to happen at Windy Holler, but I need every spare hand."

Elnora sniffed. "I'm not a field hand."

"And you won't eat like one either." Nolan passed Aynsley a bowl of peas. How had he never noticed Elnora's hatefulness? Sure, he remembered her pettiness as a young girl, but she had never been this spiteful.

Or had she?

Nolan glanced at Aynsley, who stared down at her plate, her fork suspended between her fingers as if waiting for another volley. She knew Elnora best of all. The thought made his blood heat with ire. What had Aynsley suffered at Elnora's hand?

"Papa never required me to do outside chores."

"And more's the pity. You'll do your part if you wish to remain here."

"Windy Holler is my home." Elnora smacked the table, and Zadie jumped. With a squeak, she looked up at her mother from her place on the bench.

Striving to keep his voice even, Nolan nodded. "It's all our home, and we'll work together."

"Mama is sick," Zadie said, digging a spoon into her potatoes.

Touching Zadie's shoulder, Elnora shushed her. "That was a few weeks ago, honey. I'm all better." Frowning, she met Nolan's stare. "I had a fever, but it passed."

"Then you're strong enough to help in the garden or with the housework?"

Elnora eyed the food on the table and glowered at the slice of cornbread on her saucer. "If I must."

Nolan forced a smile. "Good. We've all got to make the best of our future."

"What future?" Elnora shrugged and yanked the saucer closer. Reaching for the stone pitcher, she poured herself a cup of milk.

"Nolan, couldn't Elnora have supper like the rest of us?" Aynsley asked softly.

His heart warmed at his tenderhearted bride. How blessed he was to have her at his side. He nodded. "Of course."

Aynsley rose half-way before Elnora stopped her by raising a hand. "I'll get my plate."

Without replying, Aynsley sat once more, but Nolan noted the unease behind her serene expression.

An hour later, while Aynsley crawled into bed, Nolan dug

through his knapsack. The worn and stained canvas reminded him of the tireless miles and years he'd spent in the saddle.

Aynsley cleared her throat. "It looks like it's seen better days."

A wry grin quirked Nolan's lips. "It has seen some long ones."

"Maybe someday you can tell me."

Nolan studied her earnest face, his heart warming at the idea. "I'd like that." His fingers brushed the spine of a book, and he pulled it out. "Here it is."

"What?"

"My book of poems." When no recollection crossed Aynsley's eyes, he held it up. "Remember Longfellow's poems? You gave it to me the night before I left."

The memory dawned on her face. Judging by the way she wrenched the quilt closer, she remembered it all too well. She had cried on his shoulder, and he had nearly kissed her. She never realized it had given him the courage to believe she shared his feelings. Later, he'd written those three letters baring his heart. Her stiff, cool answer had crushed it.

He'd gone into battle not caring whether he lived or died. Somehow, he'd survived.

Aynsley spoke barely above a whisper. "I can't believe you have it after all this time."

"It's a wonder with all the places I've been. It's a bit tattered and stained, but every page is intact." Nolan stepped closer. "It's the one piece of home I carried. And the only part of you."

He watched her dark eyes widen in surprise. How was that possible after the words of devotion he'd written?

"I … I …" Aynsley bit her lower lip and darted away her glance.

Nolan swallowed disappointment but knew better than to

press further. He pasted on a smile. "I thought I'd read to you, if it's all right."

"Like old times?"

"Yes."

She ventured a look at him and dipped her head. "I've missed it. I'd like it very much."

"Well, then, let's not waste another second. Morning comes early." As Nolan carried the chair closer to the bedside, the weight on his heart eased somewhat. Maybe, in time, he'd win her.

Settling himself, he opened the book and propped his feet on the edge of the bed. He thumbed through the pages, careful to avoid anything romantic.

"Here's a good one."

The more Nolan read, the more enchanted Aynsley's face grew, her far-off gaze picturing the scenes, soaking up every word. Almost as though starved. Nolan's heart ached.

She'd said she'd missed it. He'd relived those moments dozens of times.

He read later than he intended, the light in her eyes driving him onward. Finally, when he set aside the book, he blew out the lamp and said goodnight.

Aynsley wriggled beneath the covers and fluffed her pillow. "Thank you, Nolan."

"My pleasure." He knelt and turned down the cover on his pallet.

Her shy voice drifted to him through the darkness. "Would you mind also reading the Bible to me?"

"Not at all. I'd be glad to."

"It'll be nice to talk about Scripture again."

Lying on the makeshift bed, Nolan ignored the unforgiving floor and rolled onto his side. "Maybe I'll let you read it to me," he teased. "It'd be fair that-a-way, taking turns."

Silence hung in the air. Nolan strained his ears.

"Aynsley?"

"I'd rather not." Her stiff, wooden voice belied the vibrant young woman he knew.

He'd better make amends and quick. He coughed a laugh. "I was teasing. I enjoy reading to you. Always have."

When Aynsley said nothing, Nolan puffed out a breath and cradled his head on the pillow, hoping he'd dodged disaster. After all, he hadn't been in the cavalry for nothing.

He knew when to charge and when to retreat.

CHAPTER ELEVEN

Embarrassment nipped at Aynsley while she scrubbed Nolan's nightshirt on the rub board, each stroke grinding it deeper. "He must think I'm horrible. To refuse to read," she mumbled. Everything had been like a dream until that awful moment. Reality had shattered the beauty of the scene. Elnora's taunt echoed through her thoughts. With her sleeve, Aynsley mopped sweat from her brow, imagining how Nolan might look if he knew. The shock and disappointment. Learning she'd concealed the truth from him. Though she'd never lied, she hadn't been forthright.

Whether a lie or not, the guilt remained the same.

"Lord, how can I go through a lifetime and hide this from him?" She gritted her teeth.

"Aynsley! Come quick. We need your help." Elnora jogged into the yard, dropping her vegetable basket. "Zadie has climbed into one of the apple trees and can't get down."

"Which tree?" Straightening, Aynsley draped the nightshirt over a wide stump and dried her hands on her apron.

"The oldest one. Of all the trees she could've picked." Elnora gripped her chest as several hard coughs racked her.

Without waiting, Aynsley sprinted toward the orchard. The oldest tree was also the largest, and she understood the lure such a tree had on a child. When she was a young girl, its branches were a magical place for her to dream.

As she approached, she saw Becca staring up into the limbs, her hands on her angular hips.

"Zadie Charlotte, be a good girl and come down," she coaxed.

"I can't."

The muffled whimper tugged at Aynsley's heart. How well she understood how it felt to be stuck with no escape.

"You're gonna have to go up after her, Miss Aynsley."

"Do you have any idea how many years it's been since I've climbed a tree?"

"You ain't forgot. I cain't, and Elnora ..." Pressing her lips together, Becca frowned and shook her head.

Still coughing, Elnora trudged nearer and grabbed her sides. "You've got to."

From her perch high in the tree, Zadie watched. Aynsley didn't miss the frightened look when she met her stare.

"You've put me in a fine position, Elnora," she hissed, bending over and tugging her bootlaces. "Zadie won't let me touch her, and I've got to force her to come to me."

"Just get her down." Elnora struggled for breath, her chalky face taut.

Aynsley jerked off her long socks and tucked her skirt into her belt like makeshift trousers. If Zadie had a fit, both of them could very well fall.

Becca gripped her elbow. "The Good Lord will help you. Be calm, no matter what the child does."

Reaching up, Aynsley grasped an overhead limb, put her bare feet against the trunk, and hoisted herself onto the first branch. The rough feel of the bark against her skin resurrected lost days of childhood.

"NO!" Zadie shrieked, her eyes rounding as she watched Aynsley draw closer.

"It's all right, Zadie. I'm here to help you down."

Aynsley climbed until she was within reach. Tears streaked down Zadie's cheeks as she tried to inch away.

"Hon', let me take you to Mama. You'll be safe there. See?" Aynsley pointed to the women below. "She's waiting for you."

"Darlin', do what Aynsley says." Elnora raised a hand to shade her eyes.

"Please, won't you let me help you?" Aynsley held out a hand.

Zadie's face crumpled. Flinching, she shifted, and her foot slipped. In less than a heartbeat, Aynsley swooped an arm around Zadie and crushed her close.

Tiny fists and feet barraged Aynsley's arms and legs, but she kept an iron-like grip around Zadie as she picked her way down branch by branch. The child's shrill cries rang in Aynsley's ears.

Just a few more branches, and they would be safely on the ground.

When Aynsley reached the final branch, she hopped down and exhaled a relieved breath. The next instant, Zadie sank her teeth into the tender flesh of Aynsley's shoulder, near her neck. Stabbing pain set her nerves on fire. Yelping, she nearly dropped the girl onto the ground.

Without a backward glance, Zadie scrambled toward the house as if a thousand fiends pursued her.

"That little imp." Aynsley kneaded her shoulder while squelching the sting of tears.

"How dare you?" Elnora's pale cheeks flushed.

"No, how dare you teach a child to be terrified of her own kin?" Aynsley snatched up her socks and boots. Her arms and legs throbbed in all the places Zadie had pummeled. Worse than the pain was feeling the senseless hatred of this child. No matter how her shoulder burned, Zadie's rejection stung worse.

Yet how could she blame her? It wasn't Zadie's fault.

"Miss Aynsley, let's get you to the house, and I'll clean the bite. I've got some ointment that'll fix it up." Becca swung toward Elnora, who was wheezing. "And you come rest in the breezeway. I'll fix up some honey water for your cough."

Neither of them argued as they trudged homeward in Becca's wake.

Leaving the kitchen, Aynsley stepped into the breezeway and drew a steadying breath. Becca's gentle fingers and ointment had done wonders for the pain in her shoulder. Zadie's bitemark wasn't deep, just enough to break the skin. The bandage prevented her dress from rubbing the wound and irritating it further.

Sitting in the rocking chair, Elnora sipped honey water and eyed her. Aynsley took time studying her cousin as well—her ashen face, thinner cheekbones, and shadows under her eyes. Until then, she hadn't considered it. Everyone was thinner these days.

Aynsley leaned against the back porch post, careful to avoid several of the tree knots. "Last night, Zadie mentioned you were sick, and you said you were all right. That's not true, is it?"

"She can't keep track of time. To her, a fortnight could be yesterday."

"Maybe, but I don't think that's the case."

Elnora shrugged and brought the speckled cup to her lips.

Aynsley glanced toward the front yard where Zadie played under a tree, the incident forgotten for a time. "Elnora, are you ill?"

"It's none of your business." Eyes narrowing, Elnora slammed the cup onto the side table. The liquid sloshed over the rim.

"I wish it wasn't, but since you're here, it is." Aynsley folded her arms.

"I'm fine."

"Folks who are fine don't have a cough like yours."

Flinching, Elnora sprang from the chair and approached, her fingers curled into fists. "You think you're smart, don't you?"

"No, I don't."

The words seemed to deflate Elnora as she chewed her lower lip. She pulled in a quivering breath. "I have consumption."

The admission crashed into Aynsley like a whirlwind sweeping through the valley. She blinked, her voice robbed of words.

Elnora's expression hardened. "I had no choice but to come home. Now, it's left to you to raise Zadie." Her bitter tone seared Aynsley's heart.

"Me? You might have years yet."

"I don't even have months. Weeks maybe. The doctor said so."

"No." Stumbling through the breezeway, Aynsley halted near the front porch, hidden from Zadie's eyes by the shadow of the house.

In the shade, the young girl chattered happily to the ducks and chickens rooting in the grass, unaware her world was shifting.

Elnora's footfalls padded behind Aynsley. She, too, stopped inside the shadows and watched Zadie. "After everything, I have to leave her to you."

Grief ambushed Aynsley from every side, suffocating her.

Despite all their hard times, Elnora was family. She missed the long-absent affection they'd once shared.

Without thinking, Aynsley touched Elnora's hand. "I'm so sorry."

"Hush up." Elnora swatted away Aynsley's hand, her lips tremoring. "Like always, you get everything ... even Zadie Charlotte. And I end up empty-handed."

"I don't understand." Spreading her hands, palms upward, Aynsley leaned closer, but Elnora sidestepped her.

"That's the one consolation I have." Elnora's eyes glinted green sparks. Descending the steps, she held out her hands to Zadie.

"Come, darlin'. Let's go for a walk."

With a sunny grin, Zadie jumped to her feet and joined her mother. As Aynsley watched them round the house, she felt invisible hands of despair close around her throat.

"Jealousy be a cruel bedfellow."

At Becca's soft voice, Aynsley turned. "You heard."

"Every word. Looks like we got more hard days ahead." Becca sighed, her brown eyes sorrowful. "You ain't gonna be alone, child. We'll help every way we can."

Becca held out her arms, and Aynsley stepped into them. Resting her head on the older woman's shoulder, she closed her eyes and pretended she was a child.

But reality snatched away the comforting thought.

CHAPTER TWELVE

"What happened to your shoulder?" Nolan glimpsed part of a bandage peeping from the neckline of Aynsley's nightgown as she finished braiding her hair.

Aynsley's eyes widened. "It's nothing, really."

"*Nothing* doesn't need bandages." Nolan winced at his stinging palms while he soaked them in a basin at the dressing table.

"It's only one bandage."

"Might as well 'fess up because I won't stop asking."

After crossing to the dressing table, Aynsley opened a drawer and put away her hairbrush. Nolan pulled his hands from the basin and dried them on a towel. "Wait a moment."

"Your hands need to soak. Those blisters are awful." Aynsley's dark brows nearly collided with her frown.

"Not until I see what's under the bandage." Nolan reached out, but Aynsley sidestepped him, horrified.

"No."

"Either you pull it away or I will." He used his no-nonsense voice, but it didn't quell her.

She jutted out her chin. "You'll do no such thing."

Perhaps old-fashioned begging would do the trick. "Please, Aynsley. I need to see. I want to make sure it doesn't get infected."

Nolan watched the indecision war across her face. Finally, she grimaced and fumbled with the bandage.

"All right, but Becca did a good job cleaning and dressing it."

"I've no doubt." Nolan stepped closer as she raised the bandage. Two rows of tiny teeth marks reddened the skin, bruising the tender flesh. Consternation filled him. "Did Zadie bite you?"

Her silence was his answer.

"How did it happen?"

The more Aynsley explained, the angrier Nolan grew. She must've sensed it because she talked more quickly, trying to diminish the incident.

Leaning down, Nolan inspected the wound more closely. "In her fit throwing, did she hit or kick you?"

"She did both."

"Are you bruised?"

"A bit, and I'll not show you either."

Her breathless voice brought a smile to Nolan's face, despite his concern. "A pity."

"Well." She crimped her lips together and tucked the bandage in place.

Nolan sobered and touched Aynsley's shoulders, his fingers gently cupping them. "I'm sorry Zadie hurt you, physically and otherwise."

"She's a child. She doesn't realize," she stammered.

"Even so, she should be punished."

Aynsley shook her head, her eyes pleading. "No, not on my account. I've got to find a way to reach her, especially now."

She had told him of Elnora's illness while he'd led the

mules to the pasture earlier that evening. The shock of the news had stunned Nolan.

"Even though I pity Elnora and Zadie, I won't let them hurt you any longer."

"It's beyond your help." Sadness filled her dark eyes. "But I thank you." Aynsley withdrew from his touch and nodded toward his hands. "You've got to soak them. It'll ease the pain." Whether she agreed or not, Nolan determined to shield Aynsley as much as possible. Working in the fields kept him away, but he wouldn't allow Elnora to be unkind while he was present.

He went to the dressing table and sat. Slowly, he sank his throbbing palms into the solution and closed his eyes. His battle-hardened hands were no longer accustomed to the plow, but time would cure them.

After they had been sufficiently soaked, he pulled them from the basin, and Aynsley wrapped them in a towel. Nolan watched as she carefully patted them dry.

She draped the towel on the washstand and opened the jar of ointment. "You must wrap your hands before plowing tomorrow or those blisters will tear."

"You make an excellent nurse."

A gratified look eased the tension on her face. Without replying, she dipped her fingers into the jar. "Hold out your hand."

She applied the medicine on one palm, then the other, her fingertips whisper soft. Nolan swallowed and resisted the urge to draw her close.

He cleared his throat, but the huskiness clung to his voice. "Thank you."

"You're welcome." A flush stained Aynsley's cheeks. She darted a glance at him and spun toward the bed.

"Since I can't hold a book, how about I quote some scripture from memory before we go to sleep?"

"I'd like that." After turning down the covers, Aynsley slipped onto the mattress.

Nolan pushed himself from the chair, the weariness of the day filling him, yet the sensation wasn't unpleasant. He'd much rather be weary from the field than the war.

He blew out the lamp.

"Aynsley." Elnora staggered to the end of the garden row, coughing. The hoe dropped from her hand.

Setting the scrubbing brush into the bucket, Aynsley straightened and hurried down from the back porch.

Elnora collapsed onto the ground, face forward.

"Becca! Come quick!" After reaching her side, Aynsley turned over her cousin. "Elnora, can you hear me?"

Her closed eyelids didn't move. Aynsley patted Elnora's cheek, repeating her name. Behind her, she heard Becca's swift approach.

"This oughta do." Kneeling, Becca unscrewed the bottle of smelling salts and held it under Elnora's nose. In a few moments, Elnora coughed and opened her eyes.

For mere seconds, Elnora's guileless emerald stare looked up into Aynsley's face, void of contempt, reminding her of their early girlhood. She brushed the dirt from Elnora's forehead.

Then recognition darkened Elnora's eyes. She turned her head from Aynsley's touch. "Get ... away."

Becca's wise gaze met Aynsley's. "Fetch the menfolk so we can carry her inside."

Numb, Aynsley stood and did as she was bidden. Rounding the front of the cabin, she looked up at the roof where Nolan and Eleazar were replacing the wooden shingles with new ones.

"Becca needs y'all. Elnora fainted in the garden."

Laying aside a hammer, Eleazar climbed down the ladder, followed by Nolan. "Is she conscious?" he asked as he jumped the remaining few feet to the ground.

"Yes, she is now."

"I reckon light work is too much for her." Nolan followed Eleazar to the backyard while Aynsley remained immobile as if her feet had taken root. Ever since they'd learned of Elnora's illness, they allowed her to help with easy chores. Enough to give her something to break the monotony of the day while they tended the farm.

Two weeks had passed, and the menfolk had crammed work into every bit of daylight. Plowing and planting, mending split-rail fences, and felling trees for a new barn.

The sweltering heat poured over Aynsley and prompted her feet to move. Her numbness dissipated as their voices trickled around the house. Strange how a person could feel shut out in her own home.

The strain of the past weeks drove Aynsley from the yard. Onto the dirt road she strode, caring little for potential danger. Besides, the muff pistol in her skirt pocket nestled within reach, and she wasn't afraid to use it.

Her eyes stung. Overhead, a canopy of tree branches barricaded the path from the sunshine. The air cooled and whisked the heat from Aynsley but failed to refresh her spirit.

The Hoskins' threats, Uncle Stewart's untimely death, her marriage, Elnora's homecoming, and Zadie's constant rejection—all of it was too much to bear. The scenes vividly played through her mind. Even that morning, Aynsley had offered Zadie a fried apple pie, and she'd refused, hiding behind the safety of her mother's skirts.

Aynsley had never felt so dirty.

"How long, O Lord?" The trees muffled the sound of her voice. Aynsley stumbled forward and gave her pent-up feelings full rein. She'd not allowed herself to grieve, but here in this natural cathedral made by God, Aynsley bared her heart.

She prayed for Elnora and Zadie, for Nolan, and her beloved Becca and Eleazar. Farther, she ventured into the wooded path, the internal storm driving her onward. As she talked to God, the path sloped until it intersected with the creek. Except during flooding, it babbled ankle-deep across the road.

Aynsley slumped onto a large, flat rock and brought her knees up to her chin. Wrapping her arms around her legs, she listened to the whispering waters while the rest of the world blurred from view.

How long she sat there, she had no idea.

"Hallo!"

At the woman's voice, Aynsley sprang to her feet and dashed the tears from her face.

CHAPTER THIRTEEN

Across the creek stood a lady holding a carpetbag. A small, brimmed hat shaded her features.

"Hallo! Are you lost?" Aynsley called.

"I should say not." The lady set the carpetbag down and bent to untie her shoelaces.

Transfixed, Aynsley watched as she removed her shoes and socks. Next, she hitched up her navy skirt and grabbed the luggage. The water swirled around the lady's toes as she stepped into the creek.

"Be careful, ma'am," Aynsley cautioned. "Those rocks are slick."

The lady threaded her way across as though wading through creeks were an everyday occurrence. Nary a time did she slip. When she reached the road, she stepped onto the dry rocks and dropped her skirts into place.

Smoothing them, she laughed. "I've waited for this the entire trip." Looking up, she sobered as she scrutinized Aynsley's face. "Who are you?"

"Perhaps I should ask you, since you're a stranger in these parts."

"Not a stranger, but it's been a lifetime. I'm Catherine O'Brien." She extended a hand.

Gaping, Aynsley accepted it. "You're Catherine? I'm Aynsley, your second cousin."

"I knew it as soon as I saw your face." Catherine released Aynsley's hand and gathered her close.

Her arms were warm, soft, and strangely comforting—like the embrace of a long-lost friend. Several times a year, Catherine sent letters to the family, always including a missive to Aynsley. After Aunt Eva would read it, Aynsley would dictate an answer. Catherine was one of the few who knew of her condition.

Aynsley leaned into the embrace and returned it. Catherine's shoulders trembled. After long moments, Catherine withdrew and peered closer into her face.

"You've been crying. Looks like for quite a while."

"I'm sorry." Aynsley's cheeks warmed as she racked her mind for a reply. "I needed a moment alone."

"Say no more." Catherine plucked up the carpetbag. "I empathize, especially with your uncle's passing."

"How did you know?" Surprise filled Aynsley.

"Stewart instructed his lawyer to inform me in the event of his death. With it, he sent a letter from Stewart, asking me to return to Windy Holler."

Aynsley's head swam. "To return?"

"I was raised in these parts, not in Missouri. Stewart wrote that you would need someone to help. I've no ties elsewhere, so I'm glad to come if you're willing to have me."

The kindness and concern in Catherine's gaze were genuine, and Aynsley was sick of nasty swipes from Elnora. With Nolan busy in the fields and repairing the farm, perhaps Catherine would be the buffer she sorely needed. Gratitude brimmed in her heart toward Uncle Stewart.

"I'm willing. If you don't find it to your liking, though, don't feel obliged to stay."

In unison, the women started the trek to the farm. Glancing sideways, Aynsley studied her older cousin.

Catherine's gaze bounced from one sight to another, her eager eyes probing the woods surrounding them. "So many memories here. I can almost picture Stewart dangling upside down from one of those trees."

A smile relaxed Aynsley's face. Catherine's soft voice soothed the stormy places of her spirit. "I think you might be a Godsend. Here I was in despair a while ago, and now I feel the burden is lighter."

"I've learned God's timing is perfect. Though sometimes we get in the way." Catherine switched her baggage to the other hand.

"Here, let me carry it for a bit." Aynsley tugged it into her hand. "How did you get here?"

"I came by train. A kind stranger offered to take me all the way to the farm, but I only allowed him to take me part of the way. I wanted to walk, drink in the sights, and remember."

How well Aynsley understood.

Save for an occasional remark, they ambled the rest of the way in a companionable silence. The quiet between them poured like a balm over Aynsley's soul. The sweet smells of wildflowers wafted around them like an invisible cloud of colors, and she imagined the vivid hues hovering in the air like dust.

Such thoughts she wouldn't dare utter. It was bad enough that Elnora plagued her. She didn't want to disappoint Catherine as well. Aynsley suppressed a groan. The desire to throw caution to the wind and simply be herself coursed through her veins at times like these. Bearing her condition was getting harder by the year.

Her well-meaning uncle and aunt had taught her to imprison herself. She had no idea how to set herself free.

Stepping from the shaded path, they entered the boundaries of Windy Holler. Catherine paused. Her blue eyes roved the grounds—every stump, flower, and tree—and rested on the two-story dogtrot.

Her chest expanded and fell. Reaching up, Catherine removed her hat. To Aynsley, she looked barely more than forty years of age.

The sunlight weaved gold through Catherine's strawberry-blond waves as she paused. "Stewart built it a few years before I left the holler. A new house for his bride. He certainly made it a lovely place."

"He put a lot of love and pride into it." That same stirring filled Aynsley. In many ways, she and Uncle had been cut from the same cloth.

"It shows." Catherine rested a hand on one of the railings of the split-rail fence bordering the front yard.

While they admired the place, Nolan stepped from the kitchen and headed their direction as soon as he saw them.

He scanned Catherine curiously. "Hello, ma'am."

"Hello." She extended her hand. "I'm Catherine O'Brien."

"She's a cousin," Aynsley explained.

"Pleased to meet you. I'm Nolan Scottsdale." He shook her hand and glanced at Aynsley.

Like a flame before a sudden wind, Catherine's smile faltered. "Nolan? I remember you. You were barely talking when I moved away."

"Really? That was a few moons ago." He chuckled.

"Quite a few."

Nolan reached for the carpetbag Aynsley was holding. "Welcome to Windy Holler. Are you here for a visit?"

"Perhaps more than a visit. Mr. Kirby sent a letter at Stewart's request informing me of his passing. There was a message from Stewart asking if I would return and help Aynsley with anything she needed. Other than friends, I have no family ties in Missouri, so I came."

Sympathy touched Nolan's face. "It's good of you to come."

Aynsley cleared her throat, cutting a glance at him. "Nolan and I married a few weeks ago."

"Married?" The color seeped from Catherine's face as she stared at them. "Oh my. I'm imposing, then. I should've written before coming."

"No, don't fret." Aynsley touched Catherine's elbow. "How could you know? It's very kind of you to come at a moment's notice to my aid."

"I feel the same as Aynsley. Come on to the house and refresh yourself." Turning, he glanced over his shoulder at them. "Would you mind staying in the cabin on the property? Elnora recently came home and is occupying the other bedroom with her daughter."

Aynsley noticed strained lines around Nolan's eyes. Too many changes and unexpected responsibilities in a short time weighed on him.

Catherine grimaced. "Mercy. And here I come, making things more difficult."

"Not a bit." Nolan shook his head. "You and Becca are exactly what Aynsley needs. The old cabin is a bit primitive, but it won't take Eleazar and me long to get it in shape. It's clean, and the roof doesn't leak."

Confusion crossed Catherine's face the more Nolan explained. Aynsley broke in.

"Becca and Eleazar are friends and fellow laborers. They are freed slaves who came to us when I was small."

Understanding dawned. "I see. The cabin will be fine. I remember it well. William built it when he first settled this place. I'll have the privacy I crave, and you won't be quite as crowded. I'm sorry for descending on you like this. I've created more work for you, Mr. Scottsdale."

"Call me Nolan. No need for apologies. We were planning to fix up the cabin anyhow. It's not more than a stone's throw from Eleazar and Becca's, so you'll be safe there. These parts are a bit dangerous nowadays."

"Thank you. And please, call me Catherine." She looped her arm through Aynsley's.

Not accustomed to receiving such an affectionate gesture, Aynsley wasn't sure what to do or how to feel. She offered Catherine a shy smile. "I'm glad you're here. I would like to be your friend."

"You can count on it." A tender look stole into Catherine's eyes.

CHAPTER FOURTEEN

Supper was as frosty as the untimely blight of a field in late spring. Elnora's dour silence had stilted the conversation to less than a trickle.

After dishes were washed up, Aynsley escaped the heavy atmosphere and climbed the trail to the family cemetery for the first time since her marriage.

The picket gate whined on its hinges as she entered the small spot. For a time, she stood and gazed at the plots, their plain stone markers carved with the names of those whose blood flowed through her veins.

The sweet scent of honeysuckle drifted from the vines covering one section of the fence and hovered in the air. Behind the other graves lay Grandfather and Grandmother O'Brien, both gone before she was born. Beside them, several unnamed stones marked the graves of babies who hadn't survived.

Near her grandparents' feet rested Aunt Eva and Uncle Stewart. Sprigs of grass were peeping their heads from the fresh dirt. Aynsley's heart ached. The life fading from his eyes haunted her.

Darlin', forgive me.

"For what?" she whispered. "For being noble and kind? Or for leaving me?"

Next to him was Mother. Uncle Stewart had deeply loved his twin sister. Not a day went by that he didn't yearn to see her once more, he'd often told Aynsley. His blue eyes would darken with the sadness of unshed tears.

Aynsley stepped closer and knelt at their feet. Though she couldn't read any of the names, she knew the inscriptions of each one by heart. Uncle Stewart had taught her their history.

She gazed at her mother's headstone, the plainest of all—only her name and the dates between birth and death. The letters swam, and she diverted her eyes.

"Sara. 1823-1843," she recited.

"You know these by heart?"

With a gasp, Aynsley whirled around to see Catherine standing outside the gate.

"I didn't mean to startle you. I'm sorry," she winced, looking embarrassed.

"It's all right. You may come inside if you wish. They're your kin as well." Aynsley gestured for her to draw nearer. "And yes, Uncle taught me the inscriptions."

Catherine stepped closer and studied each one, her eyes full of emotions that Aynsley understood. Love stored up and unspent on those no longer present.

Her cousin drew a breath of the sweet air. "It's peaceful."

"Yes, I come here to soak it in."

For a while, neither of them spoke while Catherine perused the resting places. Reaching down, she touched the makeshift cross on Uncle Stewart's grave.

"We plan to get a stone when time allows," Aynsley explained.

Catherine nodded. "Stewart was a good boy, a good man." Her voice thickened. "I'm glad he raised and cared for you."

"He adopted me so that I could have the O'Brien name and be a sister to Elnora. He wanted me to belong—like a daughter."

"And did you?"

"Yes."

"Judging from supper, I'd say Elnora doesn't feel the same."

Aynsley squirmed. "She doesn't. When we were children, we were fairly close, but it changed over time."

Sympathy touched Catherine's eyes. "To lose a friend is hard. To lose kin, harder still." Her eyes wandered to Sara's stone, tears shining in them. Aynsley watched a myriad of emotions cross her cousin's expression.

"You and my mother must've been very close."

"I knew her as well as my own soul."

"Uncle Stewart made her real to me. I loved his stories of her. Could you tell me yours sometime?"

A wistful smile curved Catherine's lips. "Someday, yes. It's painful for me to speak of her."

One question burned in Aynsley's heart. Something she'd never dared ask her uncle. She stared at the ground, powerless to restrain it any longer.

"Do you think my mother would've been ashamed of my condition?"

The space of several seconds passed. Catherine's shadow cast itself at Aynsley's feet. Fingers touched Aynsley's chin and tilted up her head until she looked into Catherine's eyes. Those kind, blue depths held hers.

"I can say without doubt she would never have been ashamed of you."

"I'm sending Eleazar for the doctor tomorrow. Elnora is growing worse," Nolan said, lowering his sore body into the stiff-backed chair. From the upstairs bedroom window, Aynsley viewed the flickering lamplight in her grandfather's cabin.

Her shoulders sank. "I'm sorry to hear it. What are we going to do?"

Her anxious voice made Nolan want to pull her into an embrace. "We'll hold on and get through it."

"And Zadie?" She rubbed her arms despite the warm evening.

"She's young. Her memory will fade, along with her dread of you. All she needs is time and love, and we'll give it."

Aynsley peered harder across the dark yard. "I've always envied your sunny disposition. How matter of fact you are in the middle of trouble. You make it sound easy. Like rolling off a log."

Nolan chuckled. "I'd rather do that."

Aynsley pinned him with a look. "So would I."

He could lose himself in those dark, murky eyes. Nolan sobered. "Whatever comes, we'll face it together."

"I wish I could somehow reach Elnora before ..." she shuddered.

"Aynsley." Ignoring his sore muscles, Nolan shoved himself from the seat and went to stand behind her. He circled his arms around her waist, easing her against his chest. Together they stared into the darkness and watched as the light extinguished in Catherine's cabin.

To maintain their privacy, Nolan leaned slightly toward the side table and blew the kerosene lamp out. The breeze from the open window fluttered the curtains.

"Why does Elnora hate me?" Aynsley whispered.

"I reckon she's jealous." Nolan tightened his grip.

"Why? She's intelligent and beautiful. She always had plenty of sweethearts. I'm none of those things, and I never found it easy to make friends."

"Her beauty and intellect are outward, on the surface. Yours goes much deeper. And you have a heart to go along with it."

To his wonderment, she relaxed into him. "I miss my sister. We were close until she turned twelve and I was ten."

"You want an outsider's point-of-view? I never saw it that way. You were sweet to her, but Elnora always acted superior. You were blind to her for a long time."

"Are you certain?"

"I am. Your nature doesn't see the bad in folks. Not at first." He rested his chin lightly atop her head, the silky tresses tickling his skin.

"My nature?" Sounding unsure, Aynsley stiffened in his arms and pulled away. "I suppose I am a bit naïve."

"No, that's not at all what I meant." What a dolt he was. She was putting distance between them, and he couldn't fathom the reason. "What did I say?"

"You said nothing wrong, Nolan."

He wished he hadn't blown out the lamp so he could see her face. In the dimness, she sounded weary and defeated. He rubbed his jaw. "I'm sorry."

"There's no need. I'm tired, same as you. Maybe a good night's sleep will clear my head. I should know better than to wish for anything different with Elnora." Aynsley sat on the edge of the bed and scooted farther onto the mattress.

How he wanted to assure her. To tell her he loved her, but she wasn't ready to welcome it. Nolan tugged down the covers of his pallet.

Aynsley wasn't only holding him at arm's length.

She was hiding from herself.

Viola Borden's stare burned into Nolan from across the churchyard as he helped Aynsley out of the buckboard. With a slight nod in Mother's direction, he held out his arm to his bride when her feet touched the grass.

"She looks angry." Aynsley rested her hand on Nolan's arm.

"I expected nothin' less."

Mother's face blazed as her gaze settled on Aynsley. Snatching up her skirts, Mother clipped toward the church, leaving Daniel and the rest of his brothers in her wake. Daniel caught Nolan's glance and shrugged.

"When she finds out we're married …" Aynsley tightened her fingers on his forearm, frowning.

"There's nothing she can do." As they moved forward, Nolan rested his hand on hers.

"She'll never forgive you."

"I know."

Nolan had never understood Mother's disdain for Aynsley, nor did it matter. Shoving the thoughts aside, he focused on the parson greeting folks in the church's doorway. As a circuit-riding preacher, he traveled a wide area of the Ozarks, visiting their meeting place every two or three weeks.

The bell pealed through the vale, a welcome sound to most folks. The sound would drift as far as Windy Holler, where Catherine and Becca tended Elnora. She'd spent a restless night intermittently coughing.

Nolan caught Dr. Watson's eye and nodded. He would ask him to stop by and see Elnora after services.

Ahead, the simple, whitewashed building hummed with voices. Smiles brightened the war-weary faces as the preacher shook folks' hands. One young man, presumably a soldier, clambered up the steps on his crutches. His britches were folded and pinned up at the left knee.

Sorrow stirred Nolan. What battle had stripped the man of

his leg? While they drew near, Nolan met the glances of his neighbors. Some nodded and others watched with hooded stares. He read the thoughts in their eyes.

What right did a Yankee have to be here? To be alive? *His kind*, after all, had ravaged their land. Plenty of blame belonged to both sides, but Nolan rested in the firm confidence that he'd chosen rightly.

Parson Shaw shook Nolan's hand. His weathered face crinkled with joy. "It's a blessing to see you home again. Welcome."

"Thank you, Parson." The firm grip heartened Nolan, and he returned it.

"Miss O'Brien, it's always good to see you."

"Thank you." Aynsley's quiet voice quavered slightly. "Please pray for Elnora. She's home and is ill."

"Rest assured, I will."

"Oh, and Nolan and I are married." Her lashes swept downward, her tone shy.

After the parson's hearty congratulations, Nolan led Aynsley to the last pew and they sat. She withdrew her arm from his and interlocked her hands in her lap. Near the front sat Mother with his brothers from the tallest to the shortest at age ten.

On the other side of the room, the Hoskins edged through the crowd toward a pew. Zeke and Ardy took their time eyeing Nolan. Behind them and free of his sling, Tom flexed his arm and shot a smug glance at Aynsley.

She whipped her head away. "I wish it wasn't wrong to hate some folks."

After service began, Parson Shaw announced the births, deaths, and marriages. When he mentioned Nolan and Aynsley's marriage, whispers shuffled across the room. Most people smiled their congratulations.

Not a ripple twitched Mother's shoulders. She faced the

front as though transformed to stone, and Nolan's brothers followed suit.

Aynsley raised her embroidered handkerchief to her lips and muffled her words. "You've taken on a heap of trouble, marrying me."

"And I'd do it again tomorrow." He covered her other hand with his. She cut a surprised glance at him, the doubt evident on her face.

Once the singing drifted to a close, Parson Shaw preached his sermon. His deep voice entreated the congregation to take his words to heart.

"War brings out the best and worst in men. We've seen good and bad from both sides. Not one family has escaped suffering." His dark eyes scanned the flock. "And yet, there's some who want to hold on and keep fighting—causing the sufferin' to continue. One of our brethren perished a few weeks ago at the hands of senseless violence."

The air in the building grew heavy. In her lap, Aynsley balled a handkerchief into her fist.

"Brothers and sisters, this ought not to be. God's Word says, 'The night is far spent, the day is at hand: let us therefore cast off the works of darkness, and let us put on the armor of light.' The war is over. Let us not threaten and harm our neighbors. Rather, love one another and show kindness to all of God's children."

The parson stepped from behind the pulpit and stood in front of the pews. "My views on slavery aren't a secret, and I've not been shy about it. It's an evil thing, and I'm thankful it has been purged from our land. We've all suffered. Too many have paid a terrible price. If we continue to harbor hatred in our hearts, we will destroy ourselves from within."

Wisdom tempered with sadness touched Parson Shaw's face. "Forgiveness and love come from our Heavenly Father. We can do nothing apart from Him. He alone cleanses us from the stench of hate. Live in peace and stop spewing threats. Unite with a righteous purpose to help one another as the Lord Jesus commands."

A subdued congregation exited the building a while later. The muted conversations thrummed across the churchyard.

After briefly speaking with the doctor, Nolan led Aynsley toward their rig. He glimpsed her from the corner of his eye as she walked alongside him. Through the sermon, her attentive stare had never wavered from the parson. Did the message refresh her spirit and renew her strength as it had his?

With Aynsley's hand resting in his, Nolan steadied her as she climbed into the buckboard. Behind him, a shuffling sound caught his ear.

"I thought I'd raised you better."

CHAPTER FIFTEEN

Aynsley's head jerked up, and Nolan pivoted to face his mother. His five brothers stood silently around her like sentinels.

"Pardon?" Nolan forced his stance to remain relaxed.

"You *married* her." Mother ground her teeth on the word.

"I did."

Keeping her voice low, she took a step closer. "You've shamed all of us."

Heat rose beneath Nolan's collar. "No, ma'am. You're shaming yourself, speaking this way."

"Your children will have a mother with no legitimacy."

"That's not true!" Aynsley's anguished words tore Nolan's heart. She clenched her fingers around the iron armrest.

"Take care, ma'am. You'd best leave here." His warning held a deadly calm. Mother ignored it, however.

"I was a widow with a two-year-old boy. You, Nolan. And I was engaged to be married. Her mother beguiled him, and they ran off together. Aynsley was the result, and her mother died alone and in disgrace—a fittin' punishment."

"No. No." Aynsley buried her face in her hands.

Fire raced through Nolan's veins. "Daniel, get Mother out of here before I do a fine job of disgracing the lot of you in front of God and the whole congregation."

"Come, Mother." Daniel seized her elbow. "We'd best leave."

As she opened her mouth to protest, Nolan edged closer. "Now."

Yanking her elbow from Daniel's hand, Mother wheeled away and strode toward the wagon, her head held high. For a moment, Daniel stared at his older brother, regret and embarrassment drawing his brows closer together. Ramming his hat on his head, he trudged away. The rest of Nolan's brothers followed.

Nolan sprang into the buckboard and slapped the reins across Thunder. Ever ready, the horse trotted away from prying eyes and ears.

The silent sobs of his wife robbed Nolan's breath worse than a kick to the ribs. When they were out of sight, he pulled the buckboard to a stop and gathered Aynsley close.

She crumpled against him. "I'm so sorry."

"It makes no difference to me." Nolan stroked her back. "To tell you the truth, I've always sorta suspected it."

"What?" Aynsley froze, breathless.

"You have your mother's maiden name. No one ever talked of your father."

Drawing back to look at him, Aynsley stammered, "Uncle Stewart legally adopted me so that I could share the family name and be a sister to Elnora. He said my father died while serving in the army. Scarlet fever. My mother died shortly after I was born."

"All of that may very well be true."

"And your mother," she choked. "No wonder she hates me."

"You did her no wrong. Her spite is misplaced." Nolan cupped her jaw in his palm.

"If you knew everything, you …" She squeezed her eyelids closed, biting her lower lip.

Nolan drew her against his chest once more. "Shhh. Don't torment yourself. You've done no wrong. I'm proud to be your husband."

"How can you be? I'm so ashamed." Her hands clung to his waistcoat as if it were her lifeline.

He stroked her hair, tempted to confess the truth. No matter what happened, nothing would change his love for her. Not scandal, gossip, mishap, or danger—nothing. This moment wasn't the time of his choosing, though. Those special words, uttered for the first time, shouldn't be said to allay Aynsley's grief.

"I can't begin to tell you how proud and happy I am to walk by your side."

"Well, ain't this a pretty sight."

Gasping, they broke apart to discover the Hoskins sitting on their mounts, blocking their way home.

Nolan straightened in the seat. "What do y'all want?"

"My patience is wearin' thin, Yankee. I told your gal to get rid of those no-goods."

Bristling at the insult aimed at Becca and Eleazar, Nolan grabbed his sidearm, only to be outdone. Smirking, Tom aimed the pistol and raised his brows with a challenging glitter in his eyes.

"I'd not do that if I were you. My arm's fitter than a fiddle and itchin' to take you down a peg or two."

Zeke jabbed his finger at Nolan. "I'm not looking to spill blood on the Lord's Day, but I ain't forgot our warning to Stewart O'Brien. The same goes for you and her. Get 'em out of these parts, or you'll rue the day you tangled with us."

Staring down the barrel of Tom's pistol, Nolan gnashed his teeth on the words he wanted to say. Getting killed wouldn't do his loved ones any good.

Zeke narrowed his eyes and leaned on the saddle horn. "Don't try my patience further." Beside him, Tom lowered the pistol into his holster. An unspoken, deadly vow steeled his glare.

With a tug on the reins, Zeke turned the horse and galloped away, followed by Ardy and Tom.

"He means to kill you." Aynsley touched his elbow.

"You saw it in Tom's eyes too?" Nolan urged Thunder into a trot.

"All too well."

"I reckon I'd better watch over my shoulder until the worst is over."

Aynsley shivered and angled closer to his side. "Will it ever be?"

"I'm sorry, Miss Aynsley, your cousin doesn't have much longer. A few weeks, if she takes care." Dr. Watson set his bag on the top step of the front porch and straightened.

"What do we need to do in the meantime?" Aynsley wrapped her arm around the porch post and leaned her head against it.

"If she's able, she needs to sit in the breezeway and get fresh air. No more chores."

Nolan approached from behind and stood beside Aynsley. "I should've never insisted she work."

Dr. Watson shrugged. "No need to blame yourself. It didn't hasten her decline. She needed the activity while she was able, but she's beyond it. Keep her comfortable. That's all you can do."

While the doctor and Nolan continued talking, Aynsley excused herself, an invisible burden crushing her lungs. How could she lose Elnora and raise Zadie? Her steps shuffled into the kitchen where Becca prepared a meal for Elnora. Perched on the bench at the table, Zadie rested a spoon on her mama's tray.

"There's a good child," Becca crooned. "Helpin' me get these vittles ready." She glanced up at Aynsley. "You're just in time. Can you see after Zadie's dinner?"

A frown puckered the child's mouth.

Aynsley averted her gaze from the hostile stare. "Yes, ma'am. I'll get it."

"You gotta start somewhere, Miss Aynsley. We all do."

"What would I do without you?" Aynsley met Becca's understanding look as she headed for the stove.

"You'd manage, I'd expect." Becca lifted the tray.

Zadie jumped down from the bench. "I wanna go too."

"No, you stay with your cousin. She's gonna get your stew."

The door thumped shut behind Becca, leaving Zadie and Aynsley alone. Keeping quiet, Aynsley dished up a bowl of vegetable stew and set it on the table. She forced her lips to curve upward.

"Becca's stew is the best in these parts, Zadie. Come have some."

For an answer, Zadie stepped backward until she bumped against the door. She flattened her palms against it, shaking her head.

For good measure, Aynsley sniffed it and smacked her lips. "You'll love it."

"No."

"Aren't you hungry?"

"I want Mama." Zadie's chin wobbled, her olive eyes filling.

"I know, honey. She's resting, though. Won't you eat? Mama will worry if you don't." Though Aynsley ached to gather Zadie close, she kept her arms locked at her sides.

Zadie's nimble fingers scrambled for the doorlatch. With a

downward tug, she wrenched the door open and disappeared through the gap. Her feet scuttered toward the stairs.

Aynsley knew better than to go after her. She sank onto the bench and pushed away the bowl and spoon. Moaning, she buried her face in her hands.

All tears fled, dried up in the wilderness of doubt and shame. To squeeze out a few would relieve the pain of the last several hours and days. Not even her will would grant the respite.

She rubbed her closed eyelids, Elnora's and Mrs. Borden's words reverberating through her mind like a roaring waterfall.

Were they right about her?

CHAPTER SIXTEEN

"May I come in?"

At Catherine's voice, Aynsley's head flew up. She cleared her throat and squared her shoulders. "Certainly. Are you hungry?"

"No. I'm here to see about you. Zadie came upstairs." Catherine shut the door.

Evading the perceptive stare, Aynsley picked up the bowl and went to the stove. "She didn't want her dinner."

"You needn't explain. Becca told me what Elnora did." Catherine's sympathetic voice failed to soothe Aynsley's heart. "What an awful thing to tell a child."

"Mayhap, but it's true." Aynsley emptied the uneaten stew into the pot.

"No, it's not." The next instant, Catherine grabbed Aynsley's arm and pulled her around to face her. "No, it's not."

Dragging in a sharp breath, Aynsley set the bowl on the counter. A fire kindled in Catherine's eyes as she released her hold. "Forgive me, but you must see it isn't true. There's nothing wrong with you. A blind man could see it. Elnora has browbeaten you into believing a lie."

"You're wrong. I'm not like other folks, and after today, I'm beginning to see why."

"What do you mean?"

"The parson announced our marriage to the church." Aynsley twisted her fingers. "Mrs. Borden—Nolan's mother—didn't know. After service, she confronted Nolan and said terrible things."

Catherine's cheeks blanched. "Viola?"

"You're acquainted with her?"

"We were school chums. What did she say?"

Aynsley peered hard at Catherine. If she knew the truth, would she deny it? Catherine waited, unwavering under her scrutiny.

Aynsley crossed her arms in an effort to bolster herself. "She claimed that my mother and her fiancé ran away together. Unmarried." She dipped her head. "And I am the result."

"You were never told?"

Heat scorched Aynsley's neck and face. "No. Uncle said he adopted me so I could share the O'Brien name. Mrs. Borden's words are true, then?"

"Yes." Catherine's eyes closed.

Like spurs digging into her side, the shame burrowed deeper. Aynsley slumped onto the bench. "Why did he lie to me?"

"Oh, Aynsley." Catherine lowered herself onto the bench opposite. "It's true Stewart adopted you, but his purpose was to give legality to your name."

"No wonder I was a burden to him."

"Nonsense. Stewart loved you as if you were his own. You were all he had remaining of Sara. I'm sure, beyond all doubt, he cherished you as he cherished her."

Aynsley's throat clinched tighter. "Why did Mother do it?"

A long sigh seeped from Catherine's lips. "When I see Elnora, I remember Sara."

"What?"

"Sara had a bit of a selfish streak, and she was willful." Catherine's eyes snapped like sapphires. "Though she cared for her dear friend, she wanted Thaddaeus for herself. And when Sara wanted something, nothing could stop her."

Aynsley gritted her teeth, fighting the desire to cover her ears. "Not my mother. Uncle Stewart always spoke well of her, though he didn't talk about her often."

"Stewart knew Sara's folly and tried to discourage her. I believe it was the one time he ever contradicted her. They quarreled, but Thad was more important than anything. Even honor. She disgraced the family."

Aynsley covered her face with her hands. "So that's the reason I never had sweethearts and heard folks whispering when I went to barn raisings and such. Nolan was my only friend."

"He's a fortunate young man. I can tell he loves you dearly."

At Catherine's words, a bitter laugh spewed from Aynsley. "Since we're telling the truth, I'll tell you this: our marriage is a business contract. We grew up as close friends, and that's how he wishes it to remain."

"I cannot believe it. I've seen the way he looks at you. He treats you with such care, like a treasure. I've been so happy to see it. You deserve to be loved that way, Aynsley."

"I'm so ashamed." Her eyes stung. "How could anyone love me?"

Reaching across the table, Catherine covered Aynsley's hands with hers and pulled them from her face.

"Sara's wrongs aren't yours. You're a woman of honor and strength. You possess the qualities your mother and father lacked. In their selfishness, they hurt a young, widowed mother in need of a husband and father. You've done nothing wrong."

Anguish glimmered in Catherine's eyes as she tightened her fingers over Aynsley's. "I'm sorry. The truth is brutal, but it will set you free. You can't undo the past, and it isn't your task to make others love you. Be true to God and to yourself. The rest will come in time."

Her head reeled. "I wish I could believe you. How can I be true to myself when I can't tell Nolan about my inability to comprehend a single letter in the alphabet? My weak-mindedness?"

"You're no more weak-minded than I am, and if Elnora wasn't sick, I'd give her the tongue-lashing she deserves." Catherine crimped her lips together and stood.

Another question plagued Aynsley, and she swallowed hard. Shifting from Catherine's perceptive gaze, she went to the washbowl and set Zadie's empty bowl within it.

Catherine wasn't to be fooled, however. "What are you afraid to ask?"

The words burned Aynsley's throat and clamored for release. She dared not turn around lest she lose all control of her emotions. "The way I am ... is it God's punishment?"

"No. He took Sara's and Thad's punishment at the cross. It's not yours to bear. They faced their consequences. Sara's father disowned her. She never saw him again. Besides that, she and Thad never had the privilege of raising their daughter."

Aynsley ventured a peek over her shoulder at Catherine. As though chilled, her cousin shivered. "It's difficult to speak of them this way. We'll talk more another time. You've had to bear enough for one day."

With faltering steps, Catherine padded to the doorway and stepped into the dogtrot.

Aynsley pulled her handkerchief from her pocket.

Mother's handiwork. Her fingers traced the lavender pansies in each of the three corners, her thoughts taking shape in vivid pictures.

Uncle Stewart once told her that the name *pansy* came from a Latin word meaning *remembrance*. Lavender pansies meant nobility and beauty.

Aynsley fingered the embroidered lavender *S*, her mother's initial. She averted her eyes from the symbol. Mother hadn't been noble. Rather, she'd died in disgrace, disowned and without honor.

She envisioned the red pansies of Uncle Stewart's matching handkerchief—the one buried with Mother. Red, in this case, symbolized enduring affection, an everlasting bond.

Could it not signify Sara O'Brien's shame as well? Aynsley tenderly folded the cloth and nestled it into her pocket. Had this burden weighed on Mother as it weighed on her, unworthiness compounded? At least, Mother was free of it.

If only Aynsley were also at liberty.

CHAPTER SEVENTEEN

"I'd like to come in, if you'd allow it." Aynsley poked her head around Elnora's bedroom door.

Propped on pillows, Elnora waved a listless hand. "Do whatever you please."

The wind flapped the curtains in the open window and stirred the limp, golden strands around Elnora's pale face. Bracing herself, Aynsley came to the bedside and sat in the empty chair.

For a few minutes, neither spoke. Finally, Aynsley folded her hands together. "How are you feeling?"

"About as you'd expect." Elnora spoke barely above a whisper.

"The doctor spoke with us."

"I know. What else is there to say?"

Aynsley took her chance. "Let's not part this way. We used to be so close, and no matter what has passed between us, I don't want to lose you."

"I find that hard to believe." Elnora's sandy brows rose.

"I wouldn't lie to you."

A look of disgust pinched Elnora's lips. "No, I guess not. We're beyond anything that once bound us as sisters."

"You can't mean that." Leaning forward, Aynsley scooted to the edge of her seat.

"Sometimes you are too naïve." Elnora's mirthless laugh ended on a hoarse cough. "What's done is done."

"No, it isn't. I don't understand." Aynsley reached out and covered Elnora's hand. The cool contact lasted mere seconds before Elnora snatched hers away.

"You never did." Moisture glazed her eyes. "You took everything that should've been mine. My father's love—"

"He adored you, Elnora. We all did."

As though she hadn't spoken, her cousin continued. "You took this place, my home."

"You told him you didn't want it. You married and moved to Vicksburg."

"And Nolan. Even him. I hadn't a chance whenever you were near."

A sharp pain stabbed Aynsley's heart. "You cared for him? Why didn't you tell me?"

"Because all you could see was yourself and him." Elnora pushed herself up on the pillows, the blousy sleeves of her nightgown swallowing her thin shoulders and arms.

Whispers of anger kindled Aynsley's temper, but she strove to control her tone. "But I always knew I hadn't a chance. You reminded me often enough."

"And yet you married him."

Yes, she had.

Elnora's icy gaze sparkled with a feeble sort of anger bereft of strength. The fight leached from Aynsley's spirit.

"Can't we forgive each other before it's too late?"

"I regret nothing."

"What can I do to make things right between us? I ask you

to forgive me. I never meant to come between you and those you loved." Aynsley bit her quivering lip.

Pulling in a raspy breath, Elnora jerked her stern face toward the open window. "You'll take Zadie's love too. She'll remember little of me, and I'm glad I won't be here to see it." The blood iced in Aynsley's veins. "You can't mean it."

Clamping her lips, Elnora stared ahead, unblinking.

What else was there to say? Raising a glance heavenward, Aynsley mouthed a silent prayer. *Jesus, help us.*

With wobbling knees, she stood. Her skirts grazed the well-worn floor planks of their childhood room as she stepped toward the door. Murmurs of girlhood laughter and dancing feet whirled around her like unseen ghosts. She could almost see herself and Elnora holding each other, twirling about the room.

As her fingers grasped the doorknob, Aynsley turned to look at her cousin once more. "I'll love Zadie and make sure she'll cherish your memory as I cherish my mother's. She'll love you. Even as I do. Whatever has come between us, my heart holds dear the best part of you—the sister I admired and remember. It always shall."

Save for a ripple of pain smarting her eyes, Elnora remained immobile, unmoved. "Please go."

Though she expected nothing else, the words struck Aynsley like a death knell. Her head pounded with the finality of her dismissal.

The air in the dark room swelled with Aynsley's silent sobs. Nolan was no fool. He'd cried into his pillow enough through the years to recognize a choked swallow.

He tossed aside the covers and crept to her bedside. "Aynsley," he whispered, touching her shoulder.

The bed creaked as she jumped. "Gracious mercy, Nolan. Go back to bed." She swiped her face with the sheet.

"No. Talk to me."

"I can't." Her agonized voice pained him. He lowered himself onto the mattress.

"You must. You'll be sick if you don't." When he reached for her, she shuffled to the other side of the bed.

"Don't. You shouldn't be sitting here."

Nolan captured her hand. "I'm your husband and your friend. We used to share our thoughts." When she didn't pull away, he ventured a confession. "I've missed you, Aynsley. Let me share your troubles."

He tugged her toward him. After a brief hesitation, she scooted closer and leaned against the headboard.

Relaxing, he circled his arm around her waist and pulled her closer to his side. "Tell me everything."

From Catherine's words to Elnora's rejection, Aynsley related every word, her voice hushed and distressed. While he listened, Nolan rested his head against Aynsley's.

He inhaled the scent of her hair, reminiscent of the open fields, awakening old memories. Such a fragrance made a man feel alive. All at once, love seemed possible. Nolan shook himself inwardly. Right now, Aynsley's feelings were paramount.

Her words dwindled on a shudder when she finished. "I hate for Elnora to leave this way."

"You have no control over it. The choice is hers." He stroked her side, hoping to comfort her. "You're a brave woman—a rare and beautiful soul."

She tilted up her head as though trying to see his face. "So much of life is a mystery."

"The longer I live, the less I know. But one thing I believe: God is faithful, and He is good. Our understanding is imperfect, incomplete. We're not meant to know it all."

"I suppose," she nodded. "So many things seem hidden behind a darkened glass. Like trying to see across these shadowed hills. All my life I've been looking through a lettered veil."

Puzzled, Nolan frowned. "What do you mean?"

Aynsley's breath hitched, and she fumbled with the hem of the quilt. "It's hard to explain."

"Tell me."

"I can't. In time, I will. I've poured out my soul enough for one night."

Nolan drew her closer. "I reckon you have. I'm glad you trusted me this far."

Tentatively, Aynsley rested her cheek on his shoulder. While they sat in silence, the moon inched upward through the window. The crickets chirped their late-night song.

Before long, Aynsley's head drooped heavier on his shoulder, and he realized she was asleep. Nolan nestled his head on top of hers, feeling more content than he had in an age. Home was right here.

Will she ever feel the same? What would she do if he confessed his love?

He'd charged into battle and watched his comrades fall on either side of him, yet nothing scared him more than the thought of Aynsley's rejection.

Nolan's heavy eyelids soon closed. While murmuring a prayer for every person on the place, he fell asleep.

CHAPTER EIGHTEEN

"There they is, yonder way."

Nolan followed the direction of Eleazar's gaze. On the top of a nearby ridge, three men sat astride their horses, looking over Windy Holler.

He shaded his eyes, trying to gauge their identity. "You think it's them?"

"Ain't no doubt. They've watched a bunch of times." Turning away, Eleazar continued replacing a section of chinking on Catherine's cabin.

Nolan's chest tightened. Like vultures circling overhead, they watched their prey. "No one is safe as long as they're roaming the hills."

"Especially you and Miss Aynsley." Grasping a trowel, Eleazar smoothed the new chinking with a skilled hand. "Becca and me has been talkin' on the matter. It's best if we move on. I hate the thought of leavin' you before harvest, but if we stay, there may not be any harvest left."

"And let the Hoskins have their way?" Nolan ground his teeth.

"Them having their way don't rile me none, but the

thought of them killing y'all or my wife does. I'd rather us all stay alive."

"Windy Holler is your home. You and Becca have worked and sweated for every inch of this place just as Mr. O'Brien."

"And now he's lyin' cold up yonder on the hill." Eleazar dipped his trowel in the bucket and scooped up more chinking. "Don't get me wrong. I ain't no coward. I'll fight any day. But sometimes you gotta know when to stand and when to walk away."

"True." Nolan rubbed his jaw roughly, the mid-day stubble prickling his fingers. "Don't make any decision yet, though. We don't want y'all to leave."

Eleazar paused mid-stroke and glanced at Nolan. Gloom churned in his brown eyes. "Mama gave me this name 'cause it means *God helps*. She wanted me to remember it. She told me no matter where I ended up, God would be right there even when I was sold and taken away from her. And He has been. He saw to it that my next master set me free. I cain't make you no promises, Mr. Nolan, but we'll stay as long as we can."

Both men gazed up at the ridge. The riders were gone. Stooping, Nolan dipped his trowel into the bucket and daubed the chinking into the gap.

"Your mama must've been a wise lady. It's my prayer you'll stay."

Side by side, they worked across one side of the cabin. Eleazar's baritone reverberated an old spiritual and loosened the tension pressing upon Nolan. Pretty soon, he joined the tune. Though the heat of the day progressed, a calming Presence arose with it. The furrowed lines across Eleazar's forehead shrank.

The beating of a horse's hooves neared them. After reaching for the rifle propped against the house, Nolan recognized the rider as he neared. Mitchum Kirby, Mr. O'Brien's lawyer.

"Mr. Kirby." He nodded in greeting.

"Hi, all." Kirby swung down from the saddle and tied his horse to the porch railing. "Y'all are working on the old cabin, I see."

"Yes, sir. There's lots of wear and tear on the old buildings." Nolan leaned the rifle against the house once more. "What brings you to Windy Holler this afternoon?"

"A bit of trouble." Kirby squinted closely at Nolan. "There's a lot of talk going around."

"Talk from the Hoskins?"

"Yep. Concerning Eleazar and Becca."

Eleazar set the trowel alongside Nolan's and straightened. "We saw 'em up on the ridge a while ago, watching."

Kirby rubbed the back of his neck. "They mean business. What are y'all going to do?"

"I've a mind to move on." Eleazar cut a glance at Nolan. "I hate to leave before harvest time, but I'm thinkin' it's for the best."

Nolan shoved his hands into his pockets. "And I've asked him to stay. Zeke Hoskin can't be allowed to run folks any way he chooses. He's not the law."

"I agree, but until we get the law settled here again, what can we do?" Frowning, Kirby spread his palms upward. "If they can get away with killing Stewart, they can with all of you. All they have to do is holler *self-defense*, and no one will touch them."

Silently, Eleazar and Nolan stared at each other, summing up the risks. Right and wrong didn't change with threats.

"It's a risk we're going to take." Nolan drew in a fortifying breath.

"You realize no one is going to help you."

"It's not their fight anyhow. I figure folks have had their fill of fighting."

Kirby shook his head with a frustrated grunt. "I've got

some business to settle up, but I'll do what I can. I have extra ammunition and a couple of rifles. It'll be tomorrow before I can return."

"You don't have to do that."

"Standing by isn't right. Stewart was my closest friend." A wry grin curved his lips. "He'd thrash me if he knew I'd left Aynsley to fend for herself—husband or not. And what they're doing to y'all, Eleazar, is a terrible sin."

"I'm obliged. We could use the extra help." Nolan extended his hand, and Kirby accepted it.

A soft feminine voice interrupted their conversation. "The cabin is looking much better." Catherine strolled nearer with Aynsley at her side. A large basket dangled from Aynsley's hands while Catherine carried two Mason jars filled with cold well water. Condensation dripped from the sides.

A crimson flush darkened Kirby's face, and he spun around. "Why, it's you."

Bouncing her glance from one man to another, Catherine handed Nolan and Eleazar the jars and dried her fingers on her apron. She held out her hand to Kirby. "Yes, it's Catherine. You remember me, of course?"

"I'd never forget." He captured her fingers with a quick squeeze and released it. "You've come home."

"As soon as I received your letter and Stewart's, I packed my things and headed south." Catherine perused Eleazar and Nolan's work. "Y'all have done a mighty fine job. It'll keep the mosquitoes out."

"We've brought your dinner." Aynsley eyed the lawyer curiously as she set down the basket on the porch. "Is there anything we left undone when we were last at your office, Mr. Kirby?"

"Not a thing. I was discussing another matter with your husband."

Aynsley's cheeks flamed at the word, and Nolan chewed

the inside of his cheek to stifle a grin. "I'd like to talk it over with you privately. Later."

Her color heightened. Was she thinking about their conversation last night? They woke before sunrise nestled together, her cheek resting against his chest. When her lovely eyes fluttered open wide, she had scrambled out of his arms and hopped from the bed. He had chuckled while she scowled and scolded.

Catching the hidden smirk behind his eyes, Aynsley raised her chin.

Tipping his hat to Aynsley, Kirby stepped gingerly toward Catherine. "Might I have a word with you?"

His words drove the pleasant look from Catherine's face. Kirby gave her a charming smile, but Nolan detected the gravity beneath it.

Kirby offered his arm. "Please."

"All right." Giving Aynsley an apologetic look, Catherine slid her hand through the crook of the lawyer's arm.

Tilting her head, Aynsley watched them amble toward the orchard. "I wonder what he could possibly want."

"I dunno." Nolan removed the towel covering the basket and inhaled the scent of bacon and biscuits. "They grew up together, didn't they?"

"I believe so." Aynsley set a bowl of gravy next to the basket. Next came the plate of biscuits. "You don't think Catherine might be trying to get Windy Holler, do you?"

Frowning, Nolan set the bacon beside the biscuits. "It hadn't occurred to me." He eyed them for a long moment, considering it. "I don't think so. The will makes it nigh impossible."

"I feel awful even thinking it." Aynsley shuffled her shoes in the grass.

"Don't be too hard on yourself. We've reasons enough to

suspect people these days." He touched her elbow with a reassuring pressure. "Cast it out of your mind."

Aynsley nodded.

Swiping a piece of bacon, Nolan shoved it in his mouth and glanced sideways at the pair. Indeed, what business had Mitchum Kirby with Catherine?

CHAPTER NINETEEN

The hot, sudsy dishwater swathed Aynsley's wrists as her fingers fished for a few spoons and forks. She cut a sideways glance at Catherine, who whisked a dishcloth over a plate.

"Is Mr. Kirby an old friend?"

"We grew up together. His father's farm wasn't far from my father's place." Catherine stacked the plate on several others.

"He seemed surprised and happy to see you." Aynsley washed the utensils and handed them to Catherine.

"It's been a long time." She dipped them in the rinse water.

A vague enough answer. Aynsley probed further. "I'm curious what business he had with you. Is everything all right? It's none of my business, but my manners are a bit rusty." She attempted a feeble smile.

Setting aside the spoons and forks, Catherine hesitated before meeting Aynsley's eyes. A rosy color stained her cheeks. "We discussed a few things concerning Stewart. Personal things that I'm not at liberty to discuss at the moment."

"I see." Aynsley drew out the last dish—a bowl—and

scrubbed it a little too vigorously. Had their personal discussion included Windy Holler?

"Set your mind at ease, Aynsley. It wasn't anything to cause you concern."

She jerked her face up, heat spilling onto her cheeks. One look at Catherine's discerning gaze revealed that she sensed Aynsley's suspicion.

"I'm sorry." She passed the bowl to Catherine. "I'm not myself these days. I shouldn't have pried. These past years I've learned it's hard to distinguish between enemy and friend."

"I'm your friend." Catherine touched Aynsley's arm. "And I'm your family."

The warm, motherly touch nearly unnerved Aynsley. For so long, she had held herself together, her soul churning toward an elusive peace.

The day Tom Hoskin murdered Uncle Stewart was the day her family died.

Family. Catherine was still a stranger. Elnora's homecoming dredged up Aynsley's inadequacies and failures. She hadn't bridged the gap between them. Time was careening over a precipice, and Elnora would step off the edge one day soon. All their chances to make things right would be forever lost.

"You're going to turn into a statue if you stand there long enough."

The husky timbre of Nolan's voice enveloped Aynsley like a warm quilt. Gazing across the front yard, she leaned harder on the balcony rail. The top landing separating the bedrooms was one of her favorite places, especially at night.

Starlight pulsed overhead like a million pinpricks in a dark curtain draped over the Ozarks. In the grass, crickets chirped.

Upward, Aynsley stared as though the answers might be hidden somewhere among the stars.

Nolan's steps halted beside her. "I figured I'd better check since you hadn't come to bed."

"I can't sleep."

"Care to tell a feller?" Nolan leaned on the rail, gazing across the hills. Aynsley glanced down at his work-hardened hands, strong and lean. Hands that had tirelessly worked to repair the fields and buildings. She longed to intertwine his fingers with hers, but she clung to the railing instead.

"It's too many things at once. I've not had a lot of time to grasp everything—Uncle, our marriage, Elnora's illness, and Catherine. I'm so ashamed for doubting her sincerity."

"I've had a few doubts myself."

"You have?"

"Yep, since Kirby talked to her in private."

"I mentioned it to her this evening."

Nolan glanced at her. "What did she say?"

Aynsley shrugged and dipped her head. "She was very sweet about it. She said she was my friend and my family."

Nolan nodded. "Don't be hard on yourself. Time will bear it out. Until then, we'll trust her friendship cautiously." He leaned closer until his shoulder grazed hers. "And don't forget, I'm your family too."

Aynsley filled her lungs with the night air, tasting the ethereal scents of the fields and forests. Her time with Nolan swept her to never-forgotten days she had locked away in memory. She'd believed it impossible to resurrect their friendship.

Yet here he stood. Her husband. Her family.

Would he ever be her love?

Nolan angled toward her. "Your silence is deafening."

She raised her head. "I was in awe. To think you're my family after so much time apart. When you returned, we were hardly friends. Why on earth would you want to marry me? To help? To have a farm? Perhaps both?"

A pained expression stole over Nolan's face as if a bitter memory had jabbed him. In the dim, he searched her face, working his jaw. A frustrated moan escaped his lips. "Maybe none of those."

Aynsley straightened, frowning. "Whatever do you mean?"

"I wanted to help you, and I wanted to have a farm. But that's not why I married you." Nolan pushed himself away from the railing and faced her.

Aynsley's breath hitched as she remembered the letters he'd written.

Let us not spoil our friendship with impossible dreams.

Holding up her hand, she backed away. "You did it because you pitied me? Or did you want to honor an old friend?"

He swiped a hand across the base of his neck. "As much as I respected Stewart O'Brien, I would never marry you to honor him." He stepped closer.

Though she could barely see Nolan's face in the darkness, his scowl shriveled her bravado. He towered over her, his nearness robbing her breath.

She jutted up her chin and forced ire into her voice. "I don't want your pity."

"And you don't have it." Closing the gap, he framed her face in his hands. The warmth of his fingers skittered across her skin. "You have something more, whether you accept it or not."

He captured her lips with his. At his touch, Aynsley stilled. She dared not move lest she wake. Tentatively, his arms glided around her, drawing her closer.

As though it were the most natural thing in the world, her arms circled his neck. His kiss grew more insistent, drawing a hungry response from her.

Here was home and the epitome of her dreams. To share

her heart with Nolan. The words in his letters drifted into oblivion as they held each other. His kisses spoke of a long, dry thirst—weary days and restless nights, searching for belonging.

For, dared she wish ... love?

As Nolan raised his head, a mist of confusion and yearning shone in his searching gaze. Their shuddery breaths mingled.

"Aynsley, do you—"

Frantic shouts erupted from the yard followed by the crack of gunfire.

CHAPTER TWENTY

"Get down." Nolan pulled Aynsley onto the floor. Gasping, Aynsley crawled after him across the landing, but he stopped her. "Stay there. Lie down flat 'til I return."

On his knees, he scrambled to the rear of the landing, which overlooked the backyard. A loud crackling pierced the air. Peering through the rails, he spied orange flames licking upward.

He dashed to Aynsley and pulled her to her feet. "Becca and Eleazar's cabin is on fire."

"Oh no! Nolan!" Horrified tears filled her eyes as he tugged her into their bedroom.

"You stay in here and away from the window." He yanked his rifle out of the corner. Whipping open his haversack, Nolan fished out a fistful of ammunition and pocketed them. "Wait until you hear one gunshot from me, giving you the all-clear. You can come then."

"All right." She pressed trembling fingers to her lips. "May God keep us safe."

He squeezed her hand and jogged outdoors.

The bullets jangled in Nolan's pocket as he sprinted

toward the cabin. The crackling and popping flamed louder and higher. Fire danced upon the roof and along the walls, an eerie sight that chilled Nolan's spine.

Becca's and Eleazar's silhouettes zigzagged as they beat the fire with gunnysacks. Nolan scanned the perimeter of the yard. No signs of trespassers lurked in the shadows. But he felt their eyes watching from afar. The hairs on his neck prickled.

Catherine dashed into the clearing, lugging a bucket. After whisking hair from her face, she plunged a quilt into the water. Becca followed suit.

"They used flaming arrows, Mr. Nolan. Hit the roof and sides of the house," Eleazar yelled.

Through the pulsing flames, Nolan saw the evidence of evil mischief. Aiming the gun toward the woods, he fired one shot to signal Aynsley.

Laying aside the rifle, he plucked up a gunnysack—probably one that Becca had saved from the cabin—and soaked it in the water. With firm, swift strokes, he beat the flames on the walls while Eleazar climbed onto one section of the roof that hadn't caught fire. His muscled arms wielded a sack.

Moments later, Aynsley was beating the flames alongside Nolan. The distinct smell of kerosene tinged his nose. Desperation seized his heart. No wonder they were failing to quell the flames.

The heat blasted their bodies. Aynsley's ebony braid unraveled, her long tresses swaying with each swing of the sack. On the roof, Eleazar smacked the blazing shingles, his arms glazed with sweat.

"Lord Jesus, help us," Becca cried, thrashing the flames licking up the doorframe.

It was useless. They leaped higher, endangering all of

them. Nolan thrust out his arm and pulled Aynsley to safety. "Get down, Eleazar! It's no use."

"But, Mr. Nolan—"

"Now or you'll fall through the roof." Nolan pulled Catherine away and grabbed Becca's elbow.

She lunged from his grip and flailed the blaze, her eyes wild. "No, sir! I ain't gonna lose my home."

While Eleazar scrambled down, Nolan wrenched Becca from the danger. "We can't save it. You're goin' to get burned." Though she struggled against his vice-like grip, he held her until Eleazar reached them, panting.

He hauled her against him, tears streaming down his cheeks. "Let it go, honey. We can't save it. Let it go."

Sobbing, Becca drummed her fists against his chest. "It ain't right! Them men oughta be shot down." She sagged into his chest and wailed.

Anger glinted in Eleazar's eyes, yet he said nothing while he held his wife.

Catherine staggered to Aynsley and wrapped her in an embrace. The loud snaps and hisses swallowed up the sounds of their weeping.

Nolan's chest pounded. He dropped the gunnysack and watched the inferno engulf the cabin and devour it like a living thing. Staggering away from the blistering heat, he held up a hand to shield his face.

He squinted closer at Eleazar holding Becca and noticed, for the first time, a trail of blood oozing from his friend's shoulder. "You've been hurt."

"A bullet grazed it." Eleazar flicked a glance at the wound. "Didn't have time to get a round off at 'em. Couldn't see good. Smells like they dashed kerosene against the house."

"I'd say so." Nolan plucked up his rifle and ground his teeth at the sight. The roof crashed down into the cabin, shooting embers in every direction. Clinging to each other, the ladies shrank farther away.

Rousing from her grief, Becca eyed Eleazar's shoulder. "Let's get to the big house so I can tend to your arm."

In silence, they trudged toward the dogtrot. Though the heat receded with each step, it stoked a blaze in Nolan's soul. The poisonous bite of hate and prejudice had endangered his friends and family. Disgust surged through him.

Into the kitchen they filed, while Nolan lit a couple of lamps. He ventured a glimpse at Aynsley. Soot and sweat splotched her nightgown. Mud and grime smeared her bare feet and ankles. Beside her, Catherine suffered the same state.

Enclosed in the stuffy room, the smell of kerosene trailed them and thickened. With hurried steps, Aynsley fetched a basin while Catherine thrust open the front and rear windows to allow more airflow.

"It was the Hoskins." Becca poured clean water into the basin and dipped a rag into it. She then lathered it with soap.

"There warn't nothin' we could do." Eleazar's face pinched while she cleaned the blood and grime from his shoulder.

Nolan held the lamp closer for Becca as she inspected the wound. "Did y'all see their faces?"

"We saw no one." Eleazar closed his eyes. "Didn't realize the cabin was on fire 'til the sound on the roof woke me. When we ran outside, a gun fired from the woods. Then I heard horses' hooves."

"Wretched trash. Every last one of 'em." Becca patted the gash with a towel and swiped away a stray tear with her sooty sleeve. "Lord, forgive me my anger. Can't anything be done?"

Nolan shook his head. "If y'all didn't see them, there's no way to prove it. Come daylight, I'll scour the woods and yard for anything that might point to them. I doubt it, though. They don't intend to get caught."

Aynsley stood next to Nolan. "Are you certain?"

"There's no eyewitnesses. It's their word against the Hoskins."

"And we all know that ain't gonna count," Becca growled, her eyes flashing.

"I don't think I've ever been that frightened in my life." Catherine edged closer to Becca and watched as she smoothed ointment.

For a long minute, all of them stared at each other, the ugly truth crowding around them like a dark, blinding fog.

Eleazar rolled his shoulders as if pinned down by an invisible weight. "Mr. Nolan, it's best if we move on."

"No."

All their stares veered to Aynsley. She curled her fingers into a tight ball. "Windy Holler is your home, and y'all are family. You can't leave everything you've worked to build."

The tensed furrows in Eleazar's face smoothed as affection filled his brown eyes. "But betimes it's best to walk away. We're all in a heap of danger. This cabin may well go up in flames next, and you might be killed. Maybe all of us. It ain't worth it to me."

Nolan leaned his hip against the table. "But we can't let the Hoskins have their way either. Will you consider staying longer? I'm acquainted with a judge in the next town yonder. He's a fair man, an abolitionist. He might help us."

Aynsley clasped his arm, a ray of hope in her eyes. "Yes, let's try it. Please, Eleazar, Becca, will you wait?"

Becca's hands paused bandaging Eleazar's shoulder. She cut a glance at her husband. In turn, he held her stare for a long, quiet moment. Indecision warred through their expressions. Finally, Eleazar expelled a long, weary breath.

"For a bit, I reckon."

"Oh, thank you," Aynsley choked, rushing to Becca's side, wrapping an arm around her waist. She rested her head on Becca's shoulder.

With one hand, Becca stroked Aynsley's hair before returning to her work. "I pray none of us regrets it."

"We'd better take turns keeping watch all through the night," Nolan said. Eleazar nodded his assent.

Catherine picked up the basin to toss the water outside. "If it's all right with Nolan and Aynsley, I can sleep in the parlor while y'all take my cabin."

Nolan nodded. "It's fine. You can bunk with Aynsley, since I'll be keeping a lookout. It'll be better if I sleep in the breezeway. Mr. Kirby has offered to help. We'll need the extra pair of eyes."

"Is that fine with you, honey child?" Becca secured the bandage and surveyed her handiwork.

Nodding, Aynsley flashed a grateful smile to Catherine. "Yes, ma'am. We'll see this through."

Like cockleburs digging into his feet, doubt needled Nolan. Three marksmen against three other crack shots. If Eleazar killed one of those men—

To hide a shiver, Nolan set the lantern on the table. A freeman killing a white man. Nolan's hands would be tied. Nothing he could say or do would save his friend from certain death.

What if Eleazar was right? Was it better to move on?

CHAPTER TWENTY-ONE

Through the previous night's commotion, Elnora didn't stir. Aynsley stood in the doorway as Becca and Catherine hovered at the bedside, their grim faces telegraphing a message Aynsley wished she couldn't read.

Elnora was dying.

The morning's sunrays dawned bright through the windowpanes, scattering golden light around the room. It didn't seem right, somehow.

The glow gilded Elnora's fair locks lying skewed across the feather pillow, accenting the hollows of her gaunt cheeks, her face like a porcelain doll. Far too lifeless and cold. Elnora's breaths shuddered, the sound fracturing the heavy silence. Aynsley resisted the urge to cover her ears and run from the room.

In one corner, Zadie ministered imaginary hurts to her ragdoll, her sweet murmurs tearing at Aynsley's heart.

Becca's hushed feet moved toward Aynsley. "You got to send for the preacher and the doctor."

"I'll go." With Nolan and Eleazar working in the back field, it would take too long to fetch one of them. After venturing one more look at Elnora, she rushed into the yard below.

Saddling Thunder didn't take long. Aynsley ran her fingers over his neck. "Will you trust me, ol' boy?"

The Morgan snorted a gentle breath and nuzzled Aynsley's fingertips. A good sign. She hoped Nolan wouldn't mind her taking him. Thunder was the quickest horse on the place.

She swung into the saddle astride, caring little for conventions. Cramming a hand into her pocket, she checked the Colt pistol to make sure it was secure. After last night, she had decided the muff pistol wasn't enough.

With an urgent tap of her heels, Aynsley set Thunder into a gallop. Her navy dress rippled down both sides of the ebony stallion and across his rump. Down the road, his hooves rumbled, trailing a dusty path in their wake.

Aynsley leaned forward into the wind. Though it wrested loose the strands of her hair from its pins, she relished the swift waves brushing her face. It tasted like freedom. To be free from rifts, sorrow, and loss. Not to mention her shame.

Time would steal away reconciliation with Elnora forever.

Intent on her task, Aynsley thrust the thought to the corners of her mind. "Only see, don't think," she whispered.

Onward, Thunder carried her through shadows dappling the road and shallow, gurgling creeks.

After telling the preacher, Aynsley steered Thunder in the direction of Dr. Watson's place. A half-mile passed before she saw a rider coming from the opposite way. Trepidation coiled around her.

Tom Hoskin.

She hardened her expression, concealing all trace of disquiet, her fingers closing around the Colt in her pocket.

He veered his horse into the middle of the road, leaving Aynsley no choice but to stop. On either side, the thick forest barred her way.

Tom sneered. "Where are you headed, Mrs. Scottsdale?"

"To Dr. Watson's."

"Someone get hurt?" A surly grin split his mouth. "Heard there was quite a fire at your place last night."

Aynsley ignored his remark. "Elnora is dying."

Not a trace of empathy passed Tom's face. He spat tobacco juice on the ground. "It's kinda stupid for your husband to let you roam around alone. A pretty filly like yourself might get a bit roughed up somewhere."

Without a blink, Aynsley raised the Colt. "Move out of the way."

Darting up hands in mock surrender, he guffawed. "Let it never be said a woman killed Tom Hoskin."

"If you don't move, I'll extend the same mercy you showed my uncle."

Tom's eyes narrowed. The smirk receded from his face as he closed his hands around the reins. "You'd best get a civil tongue in your head, or I'll learn ya a lesson you won't ne'er forget."

Aynsley cocked the hammer with her thumb.

Cold hatred glittered in Tom's eyes, but she stiffened her spine. Digging his heels into the horse's flanks, Tom galloped past her.

Aynsley watched until he was out of sight. Only then did she lower the hammer.

"Why didn't you come to the field? I would've gone for them."

Aynsley winced, not from Nolan's gentle hands capturing hers but from a hasty decision that could've ended badly when she encountered Tom. "I thought I'd be wasting precious time for Elnora."

"Thunder gave you no trouble?" Worry entrenched crow's feet around Nolan's blue eyes.

"Not a bit. We got along famously." Biting her lip, she hesitated. "Tom Hoskin was another matter, though."

His face paled while she recounted the incident, his grasp tightening. Lowering his voice to an insistent whisper, he leaned closer. "Please never leave without me again."

"I'm sorry." Her chin tremored, and his fingers immediately caressed the spot.

"No, don't be. You wanted to help Elnora, but I don't want anything happening to you."

The world around them faded as they lost themselves in each other's gaze. Aynsley's pulse galloped. What was happening between them? Nolan had sworn friendship, and he never broke his word.

Or was he? The memory of their shared kiss heated her cheeks. Would he feel the same if he knew her secret?

The door hinges groaned as Dr. Watson stepped onto the landing. Before tearing his gaze from hers, Nolan gave her chin a gentle tweak. Together they faced the doctor.

"I remember the day Elnora was born." Dr. Watson rubbed his neck. "She won't see another dawn. I'm sorry."

A stabbing pain throbbed Aynsley's eyes. "How can we make her comfortable?"

"I've left some medicine on the dressing table. She can have it every few hours. It will help her rest."

With a somber face, Nolan gestured toward the stairs. "Thank you, doctor. Would you care for a cup of coffee?"

"I could use one. I'm obliged." Dr. Watson's weary steps lagged behind Nolan as they headed for the kitchen.

Hugging herself, Aynsley stared at Elnora's door and tried to picture what Becca and Catherine were doing inside. Was Elnora awake? Had she thought of her? Asked for her?

She choked on a swallow and raised her hand to knock.

After several shuffling sounds, Becca opened the door. The strain of the past twenty-four hours ringed her eyes.

"She ain't asked for you yet," she whispered. "I finally mentioned it, but she never answered."

"Mayhap she didn't hear."

"She heard." Becca looked over her shoulder. "Preacher's talkin' to her. I'll do what I can. When you get a chance, send Mr. Nolan to fetch Zadie Charlotte."

Boosting herself on her tiptoes, Aynsley peeped into the room. Elnora's gaze focused on Parson Shaw, her eyes intent. The parson took her hand. Her quick, shallow breaths raised the hair on the back of Aynsley's neck.

She veered away from the scene, but Becca grasped her elbow. "I'll try to ask her again."

Aynsley shook her head. "Leave her be. My presence would disturb her. Let her go in peace."

CHAPTER TWENTY-TWO

Nolan straightened his stiff, sore muscles and cast aside a charred tin can. Under an oak, Zadie sat rocking her doll, her curious stare following them as they shuffled through the remains of the cabin. When she caught his eyes, she tucked her chin. Sympathy tugged his heart. Such a sad, doleful face. Too much for a child so young.

"It's a cryin' shame that child won't let Miss Aynsley near her." Eleazar glanced at Zadie, a slight frown pinching his mouth. "She'd love her through this trouble."

"How or when will that ever happen?"

"You got brothers. You know how children be. Keep being gentle." Eleazar sifted under a few boards and pulled up an iron cooking pot. "She'll come around, cravin' for a papa and mama more than a doll." He dropped the pot beside a pile of odds and ends they'd managed to salvage.

Nolan scraped a palm across his jaw, watching the little girl. A papa and a mama. "I'd never thought of it."

Was it possible to raise Zadie as their daughter? Would she accept it? Though prim and proper, she possessed a wild streak in need of taming. Could love make them a family?

As Nolan bent to retrieve a few gritty dishes, he remembered the look in Aynsley's eyes when he'd kissed her. The way she'd returned it. His neck burned, and hope ignited. *Though I hold you in the deepest regard, I could never promise my heart.* The words of her letter stampeded into his musings and across his aspirations. Long ago, he'd misinterpreted her demeanor, believing she shared his feelings. Even now, he glimpsed those same emotions beneath her composed exterior. Last night, when he'd held her in his arms, he'd never been so sure of her love.

Just as he'd felt before he received the letter that shattered his heart.

Would they ever be a family—give Zadie brothers and sisters to love? Or was he setting himself and Aynsley up for heartbreak?

Patience. I have a lifetime to try, if the Lord wills.

Unease for Elnora added to the taut muscles across his neck. Her earthly lifetime would soon sever its grasp on her soul. Glancing westward, Nolan noted the sun's waning trek across the sky. *Father, have mercy on her. May she find grace before she crosses to the other side.*

The sun lengthened its journey farther west while he and Eleazar toiled through the blackened grime. Very little remained. In the shade, Zadie sang, cradling the doll close to her chest. Her fairy-like voice drifted over them, enchanting, perfectly pitched.

"Jesus loves me—this I know
For the Bible tells me so;
Little ones to Him belong,
They are weak, but He is strong."

Nolan and Eleazar paused and listened.

"Jesus loves me—loves me still
Though I'm very weak and ill;
From His shining throne on high
Comes to watch me where I lie."

Zadie's clear voice dwindled into a hum. Unaware of their stares, she smiled down at her baby and kissed its cheek.

Nolan's breath tripped on something in his throat. Eleazar rested a hand on his shoulder, his voice low.

"Miss Aynsley's coming yonder."

Though the skirts hid her halting steps, they dragged like heavy fetters around her feet. When she neared, she raised her head and met his glance, her dark, luminous eyes a stark contrast to her chalky face. He needed no words to discern her bleak expression.

Nolan opened his arms, and she walked into them. Shuddering, she hid her forehead against his chest and wrapped her arms around his waist. He pulled her closer.

Beside him, Eleazar stroked Aynsley's hair. "Send comfort to us, O Savior, and strengthen us for the days ahead. We ask your mercy on Zadie Charlotte. Help her to accept our offerin' of love."

Zadie's watchful, bright eyes scrutinized them. Pulling away slightly from his embrace, Aynsley looked up at Nolan.

"Will you take Zadie to the orchard and explain things? She likes it there."

"I surely will." He skimmed his lips against her forehead before releasing her. Tentatively, he stepped over to the child and held out his hand.

"How 'bout a walk to the orchard, Zadie?"

With an uncertain frown, she smoothed her doll's hair. "But Maggie's sleepin'."

"Then let her be. She'll be safe 'til we return."

"I s'pose." After checking the towel swaddling Maggie,

Zadie nestled the doll between two tree roots. "There. She'll be snug, won't she?"

"Very snug, darlin'. Come along."

As her tiny fingers closed around his, anxiety cinched a cold grip around his chest, and he sought out Aynsley's face. She stood with a hand covering her mouth, watching them. He offered her a sad smile as he led away the child.

Never had the path to the orchard stretched so far.

Though the trees obscured her view of the orchard, Aynsley stared into the canopy while leaning against the post. A breeze flitted through the landing, but she hardly noticed. Nolan and Zadie had been absent for a long while.

Straining her ears, she listened for sounds of wailing, but birdsong echoed through the branches instead. Her heart quivered, nigh to bursting.

The door to Elnora's room snapped shut, and Becca approached. "We're almost finished getting Miss Elnora ready for the burying. Eleazar will have the coffin built later tonight."

Unable to speak, she nodded, closing her eyes against the sounds of Eleazar's hammer in the yard.

Lifting her apron, Becca patted dry the sheen on her face and neck. "I need to tell you something."

"I can't bear to hear it."

"You can. Maybe it'll help, but maybe not."

Aynsley dug her fingernails into the rail, waiting.

"Preacher spoke true words to her. Said no one harborin' hate or unforgiveness could enter God's heaven. Told her Jesus loved her and could erase every stain if she'd allow it. He read the Good Book, took her hand, then prayed. Miss Elnora's lips moved, but I couldn't hear what she said. After he left, she slept awhile then woke." Becca fought to keep her voice even. "She mentioned you."

Aynsley jerked her face toward Becca. "What did she say?"

Shifting her eyes to the trees, she gulped air. "Miss Elnora said to tell you goodbye."

Blinking, Aynsley shifted closer, intent on Becca's next words.

"She spoke again, but her words faltered. So's I asked again. She tried to tell me, but then the light left her eyes, an' she was gone."

A terrible sort of desolation, a feeling of finding something only to lose it, engulfed Aynsley. Reaching out, Becca stroked her hand. "Her eyes spoke her regrets."

Turning her palm upward, Aynsley clasped Becca's fingers and soaked up the comforting touch.

Blue, hazy twilight shrouded the landscape, deepening as the sun slipped farther behind the ridges. Along the edge of the woods, lightning bugs flickered among the trees.

"Here they come." Aynsley strained her eyes in the dim light.

Nolan ambled up the path. Cradled in his arms, Zadie lay with her face tucked in the curve of his neck, looking more like her doll than a growing girl.

The sight pricked Aynsley's soul. How she longed to rush down and take Zadie into her embrace.

"Poor child," Becca murmured. "You'll manage it, Miss Aynsley, with the Good Lord's help."

Though Aynsley opened her mouth, no words came. Soundlessly leaving Elnora's room, Catherine joined them. "I've finished my part, Becca. I would've arranged her hair, but she wanted you to do it." Fatigued lines thinned her lips.

"I'd best go do it then, so's she'll be ready for the menfolk to lay her in the coffin." She withdrew her hand from Aynsley's. "There'll be a mess of folks here tomorrow."

As Becca returned to the task, Catherine sagged against the post, her arm brushing Aynsley's. "I'll do whatever I can to help you with the little one."

Aynsley gave her a faint-hearted smile.

Empathy filled Catherine's eyes. "Try not to fret. She'll come around."

She prayed so. A heavy grief worse than losing Uncle Stewart surrounded Aynsley, choking her. A long, uphill climb waited, a journey that life compelled her to take.

Would she fail those who needed her?

"Is this how Uncle Stewart felt when he took me to raise?"

The contours of Catherine's face tensed. Gliding her fingers over her cheek, she pulled in the evening air between her lips and released it slowly. "I wasn't here then, but I know he loved you as his very own."

Aynsley flattened a palm against her chest, the burden too heavy for words.

Seeming to understand, Catherine drew her into her arms.

Closing her eyes, Aynsley rested her cheek on Catherine's shoulder. A calm hush descended upon them while they stood in the gathering dusk. They needed no words for this moment. Their hearts forged a bond.

CHAPTER TWENTY-THREE

"I'll return by sundown." After setting his foot in the stirrup, Nolan swung up into the saddle. A worried look tensed Aynsley's face as she glanced around the place. He reached down and took her fingers in his. "Kirby's here. I doubt there'll be trouble today."

Aynsley's stare settled on the hillside graveyard where they'd buried Elnora that morning. "I'm worried more for you than us."

"I'll be watchful." His stiff lips, like a rusty hinge, cracked a smile for her sake. "The Lord has seen me through this far, and I figure He'll keep me the rest of the way. I'll make it home."

Releasing his fingers, she crossed her arms as though shielding herself. "See that you do."

Pressing his knees into Thunder's side, Nolan set off for Judge Morris's place. A twinge of relief tempted him to relax, since the judge's home was in the opposite direction of the Hoskins' place. He'd not let his guard down, though. Besides the Hoskins, bushwhackers still roamed the mountains and vales.

Thunder, too, pricked his ears, his nostrils flaring as he trotted along the path. Nolan patted his neck and murmured comforting words. The Morgan could smell trouble even better than he. "I trust your judgment better than my own, ol' boy. Say the word, and we'll return to the holler."

More than once, Thunder had saved his life. Nolan massaged a scar, an exit wound above the horse's withers, recalling when the stallion had reared up and taken a bullet meant for him. Afterward, the doctor had stitched Thunder and declared him worthy of a commission.

Blinking away the memories, Nolan flexed his fingers and eased his grip on the reins, choosing to focus on this day.

A large crowd of neighbors had assembled early, bringing a wide assortment of vittles and proceeding to the graveyard to pay their respects. Strangely, Catherine had shut herself away in the bedroom, claiming a headache. She didn't come downstairs until after the last neighbor had ridden away. Her pallid face and bloodshot eyes testified to the truth of her claim.

Yet, suspicion nipped at Nolan despite Catherine's seeming devotion to their family. She'd worked alongside the women, literally fought fire, cared for Elnora until her last breath, and filled a void that Aynsley sorely needed. In some ways, Catherine fit in too well.

She's hiding something.

Nolan scrubbed his palm across his forehead, irritated with himself. Mayhap the war had mangled his trust in folks. He had no reason to distrust Catherine.

Yet, somehow, he did.

Onward through the miles he traveled, his thoughts roving to the morning funeral—Zadie's hands locked around his neck while she hid her face, the absence of his mother and brothers, the singing cascading down the hillside into the valley, Parson Shaw's words, and Aynsley's bleak, tearless face. It pained him. She'd clung to his hand throughout the service.

I'd rather see her weep than watch her silent, stark grief.

Things between her and Elnora remained a mystery to him. Though he knew jealousy laid at the root, Aynsley had never fully shared their troubles. She'd hardly understood the cause herself.

Whatever it was, Aynsley must move forward and put it behind her. Their personal civil war was over.

When he rode into the judge's yard, he scanned the place— still as tidy as he remembered it, despite the peeling whitewash on the house, neglected in recent years. On the front porch sat Judge Morris in a straight-backed chair, whittling on a piece of wood.

"Hallo!" Nolan reined in Thunder.

Jerking up his head, the judge squinted with a frown. He set aside his knife and wood before rising. "What can I do for you?"

"Judge Morris, it's been a while." Nolan lowered himself onto the ground.

A wide smile tipped up the corners of the older man's bushy mustache. "Nolan Scottsdale, come on up here and let me get a look at you."

Judge Morris pumped Nolan's hand, chuckling. Nolan basked in the friendly welcome. "It's good to see you, sir."

"Even better to see you. Glad you made it home. Come and sit." Judge Morris gestured to an empty chair next to his. "You caught me red-handed, idling my time away."

"Looks more like you've been whittling to me."

Quiet pride flashed in the judge's eyes. Winking, he picked up the knife and wood. "I need a new pipe. The old one's worn out."

"It has the makings of a handsome one."

"By the time I'm finished, you won't find a finer one this side of the Mississippi."

"I'm sure of it."

Sobering, Judge Morris studied Nolan for a silent moment. "Well, we've won the war. The cost was high, but we persevered."

"I pray we never face years like it again."

"Not in my time, at least." The judge grunted. "What brings you to these parts?"

Nolan rubbed his hands together. "A bit of trouble."

"Let's have it."

After relating Stewart O'Brien's death, he detailed the Hoskins' demands and threats, their burning of the barn and the cabin. With each event, Judge Morris's pleasant expression shrank into a grim scowl. He shoved aside the wood and knife onto a side table.

"These are nasty days, Nolan. I don't need to tell you the lawless deeds we've endured. A band of thieves can ride into the yard and take anything they want."

"Governor Murphy has called for peace and reconciliation."

"The governor's words are as useless as Confederate money. 'Til we establish law and order, we fend for ourselves."

Nolan leaned forward, resting his elbows on his knees. "I came to ask for your help."

Judge Morris's eyebrows arched. "My help? In what manner?"

"There's got to be a way to stop the Hoskins from harassing us. A legal way."

"There's no way."

The answer stole Nolan's breath. "They can't be allowed to terrorize citizens. I believe you feel the same as I do. Why can't you help?"

A heartsick grimace aged the judge as he pinned Nolan

with a stare. "I gave five sons to save the Union, and none came home. My youngest boy was too young to serve. He was bushwhacked a month ago." He balled a fist and hit his knee. "Because I'm a Unionist and a judge."

Dropping his gaze to his feet, Nolan squeezed his eyelids shut. "I'm sorry, sir."

"Those scoundrels dropped his dead body at our doorstep and warned me to keep my business at home. I've plenty of Confederate friends who'd never do such a thing, but these men are savage—indiscriminate killers. I've my wife and daughter left. I can't allow them to be killed or attacked, if you get my meaning," he hissed.

Nolan nodded. He knew exactly, and the idea made him ill. "I apologize for troubling you."

Regret glittered in Judge Morris's eyes. "I'm too old to fight. The war's been won, but it's taken nearly everything I held dear. And we're not the only ones."

Nolan's chest tightened. "I hope you'll accept my condolences and give them to your wife. I'll be praying for y'all." Rising from the chair, he held out his hand.

The judge stood and accepted it in a tight grip. His eyes misted. "Fight 'em. Do whatever you must to protect your loved ones. No one will fault you."

"I will."

"I'm sorry, son. Order will return, but healing takes precious time."

Nolan released his hand. "You don't owe me an apology, not by a long shot. I appreciate you hearing me out."

After mounting Thunder, Nolan saluted the judge.

Over the hills, dark blue-gray clouds loomed. A silver lightning streak highlighted the ridge, a soundless summons to battle.

He'd do what he must.

No matter the cost.

CHAPTER TWENTY-FOUR

The afternoon thundershower had soaked Nolan to the skin, plastering his sandy hair to the sides of his face. After returning from the judge's place, he'd dashed into the makeshift lean-to and unsaddled his horse.

Aynsley watched from the shelter of the porch as sheets of rain pelted the yard. By the time Nolan sprinted to the house, rivulets streamed down his chest and legs as he skipped up the steps two at a time. The sky rumbled and rattled the windows.

"There are dry clothes across the bed." Concern thickened her voice as she followed him farther inside the breezeway.

"Thanks." He raked the hair from his forehead and squinted, his eyes undoubtedly adjusting to the dimness. His glance snagged on Catherine and Mr. Kirby standing next to her. A slight frown puckered the skin between Nolan's eyebrows, but it dissolved as quickly as it appeared. Was he still suspicious of Catherine?

Aynsley cast a furtive look at her cousin, but Catherine hadn't seemed to notice. Sweeping his hand down his sleeves and pants, Nolan whistled. "It about got the best of me. Y'all give me a few minutes to change."

When he was gone, Aynsley wandered over to a rocking chair, the damp air gusting past her as it pummeled the front of the house. "It'll be a wonder if he doesn't catch cold."

"It's a warm day, and I'm sure he's accustomed to suffering all kinds of weather. He'll be all right." Mr. Kirby offered her a reassuring smile while he and Catherine returned to their chairs.

Settling against the seat, Aynsley forced herself to relax. The last thing she needed was to put Nolan to rest in the graveyard next.

"The Lord didn't bring Nolan through the war to take him away from you." Catherine's soft voice poured solace over Aynsley's soul like an anointing oil.

The fringes of a smile curved her lips. "How did you know what I was thinking?"

"You spend a lifetime never knowing some people. And with others, it takes a few moments to feel you've known them forever. You have that gift, Aynsley. That's how I know."

Gift? No one had ever said such a thing of her. She didn't possess any gifts.

Nolan soon returned, dry and fresh, his bare feet padding down the stairs. Forgetting herself, Aynsley admired him—his pleasant face, his broad, lean chest, his assured gait as he strode toward her.

Then her eyes met his. A heated flush scorched her cheeks. He'd caught her, and the gleam behind his stare sent her pulse skittering. Snapping her gaze away, she squirmed.

"How'd the visit go?" Mr. Kirby stood half-way to offer his seat, but Nolan gestured for him to keep it.

"Not as I expected." Nolan moved toward Aynsley and stood next to her chair. He rested his hand on her shoulder, the warmth soaking through her blouse, instilling a sense of belonging she'd never experienced and hardly understood.

"What happened?" she asked, schooling her tone to remain unaffected.

"He can't help." Nolan's face darkened.

"Can't or won't?" Intent, Mr. Kirby scooted to the edge of the seat. Sitting next to him, Catherine raised a hand to her mouth with an anxious gasp.

"A bit of both. I don't blame him. His hands are tied." The muscles in Nolan's jaw knotted as he clenched his teeth. "The war will never be over for some."

As he explained their conversation, his hand tightened on Aynsley's shoulder, the tension spreading across Nolan's face. His fingers slid away, and he slumped into the empty rocker beside her. For an instant, lightning blazed the sky and illuminated the breezeway.

Mr. Kirby's brow furrowed. "I can't say I'm much surprised. Lawless men have been accustomed to getting their way for too long."

"It's got to stop somewhere."

"The question is when and how. Either way, it won't be soon."

Nolan expelled a breath. "Nope. It's up to us to fend for ourselves."

"I've already been warned to steer clear of Windy Holler." Mr. Kirby stood and shoved his hands into his pockets. "Seems the Hoskins have been watching me come to and fro, a bit too much for their liking."

"Whatever for?" Catherine demanded, seizing the armrests. Her face, already strained from the ordeal of the past few days, sapped of color.

"They're many things, but stupid isn't one of them. I'm your nearest neighbor, and they can see I'm armed for a fight."

Nolan frowned. "You'd best stay put. This is not your fight."

Nonchalant, Mr. Kirby shrugged. "I don't scare easy. It's all our fight, Nolan. It has to start somewhere."

"Or end." Aynsley rubbed a sharp pain stabbing her temple as the thought of another ensuing fight brewed. Uncle had been taken the first round. "Will any of us be spared by the time it's all over?"

"Only the Lord above knows." Mr. Kirby bowed slightly to the ladies. "I've my evenin' chores waiting, but I'll return in a while."

"Perhaps Eleazar should go too." Catherine stood, glancing at the kitchen. "I'm sure he'd be willing."

Mr. Kirby shook his head. "If we were caught, it would go badly for him. We're both safer if he stays here." His mouth curved upward. "I've tangled with bad men before. I'll not be careless."

As Nolan accompanied Mr. Kirby to his horse, unease hovered over Aynsley like a thick haze. The rain-cooled draft whisked through the dogtrot, fluttering her skirts and sending shivers across her body.

A few hours later, after chores, Nolan entered the parlor. Aynsley looked up from her needlepoint. Beside the empty hearth, Catherine rocked Zadie and hummed a lullaby. Careful not to disturb the child, Nolan treaded softly across the rug.

Zadie's long eyelashes fluttered and brushed against her rosy cheeks. Her ringlets dangled and swayed with the rocking. Her tiny, bare feet peeped from beneath her nightgown. Aynsley's heart wrenched against her ribcage. Such a motherly picture—Catherine's head bent low, the soothing melody from her lips, and Zadie's sweet innocence. All trouble absent from her tranquil brow.

Aynsley's empty arms ached both for the child and the mother she'd never known.

Touching her arm, Nolan cleared his throat, and she jerked to the present. Worry lines furrowed around his mouth.

He bent close to her ear. "Kirby should've already returned. I don't like it. I'm going to check."

Alarm shot through her. She closed her fingers around his sleeve. "Are you sure?"

"Something's not right. Waiting might be the difference between life and death." His hand grasped hers, and he tugged it, urging her to stand. "See me out."

Behind them, Catherine's humming faded as they stepped onto the porch. Nolan's somber gaze met hers. "If I'm not here in an hour, send Eleazar."

"Oh, Nolan." Her knees trembled.

"I'll be careful, but if there's trouble, I might need help."

Aynsley forced courage into her voice. "I'll wait out here in case I hear shots."

"My sweet soldier." His fingertips skimmed her jawline. "Always on the lookout." An instant later, he crushed his lips to hers. They were insistent and warm, hinting promises she shrank from believing. Even though the truth stood between them, even if he might feel differently should he discover it, she surrendered herself to his caresses. Like an iron band, his other arm rounded her waist and pressed Aynsley close. When he wrenched his lips away, his dark and tumultuous eyes searched the depths of hers.

The next second Nolan was striding toward Thunder who waited, stamping his feet.

CHAPTER TWENTY-FIVE

Out of sight of the house, Nolan tied Thunder to a branch and crept closer to Kirby's yard. He crouched behind a bush, hidden in the evening shadows. Silence pervaded the place. Much too quiet.

He didn't like it. A large knot tightened in his stomach as he scanned every nook and cranny in sight. The outbuildings, the side yard, the murky porch, the trees. The kitchen window glowed with light.

His thumb eased back the hammer of his drawn pistol, and he sprinted into the shadow of a tree. Waited. When nothing moved, he sprang toward the dark silhouette of the house and pressed against the siding. Listened.

A muffled moan inside the house squeezed the breath from Nolan's lungs. Darting a glance in every direction, he sidestepped the length of the house and eased around the corner. Another groan reached his ears. Up the back steps he crept and peered through the window. Kirby sat hunched over the table, writing in agony. No one else was in sight.

Closing his fingers around the knob, Nolan opened the door. A blast of heat from the kitchen stove smacked him across the face. With his gun still drawn, he stepped over the threshold, listening for any other sounds in the house.

"Kirby," he hissed.

The man groaned. "They're gone."

Snapping the door shut, Nolan rushed to Kirby's side. "What happened?" Kneeling, he surveyed the damage. A large lump bulged from the side of Kirby's face, and blood oozed from his nose. Kirby peeked up at him through his swollen eyelids.

Horror galloped through Nolan's veins when he viewed Kirby's hands.

From the palms to the fingertips, blisters bubbled on top of the crimson flesh.

Agonized tears poured down Kirby's face. "They were waiting in here the whole time. After I finished the chores, I came in to wash up, and …" He gasped when he moved his hands. "They said they'd warned me for the last time. They'd lit the stove, had it blazing hot."

Closing his eyes, Nolan gulped down the bile surging up his throat.

"They held my hands to the burner." Kirby gritted his teeth.

"Those devils. How long have they been gone?"

"About an hour."

Grabbing a dishtowel from the counter, Nolan dashed outdoors to the nearby well. After cranking up a bucketful of cold water, he soaked the towel and brought it into the kitchen.

"I'm going to wrap your hands and take you home." Quenching his own tears at Kirby's agony, Nolan wound his hands in the cold cloth.

"Thank you, Nolan," Kirby murmured.

Unable to speak, Nolan shut off the stove's air vents to

extinguish the fire. Helping Kirby to his feet, he led him outside and hoisted him onto his horse.

"Can you hold to the saddle horn while I lead your horse?"

Kirby nodded, his eyelids now swollen shut. "As long as I have this wet cloth, I can grip it. I'll do what I must."

After untying Thunder, Nolan held the other horse's reins, and together they made the mile-long trek to the hollow.

Thunder swiveled his ears at every sound in the awakening forest. Nolan stroked his sleek neck, thankful the faithful stallion didn't spook easily. Farther in the trees, a pair of owls hooted to one another.

Kirby moaned, igniting Nolan's fury. Tightening his fingers around the reins, he muttered a prayer for their protection while grappling against his murderous thoughts.

Lord, forgive me, but I want to kill every one of 'em.

How many men he'd killed during the war, he didn't want to know. Every time the memories teemed, scenes and faces drowning him, he prayed for their families and asked forgiveness. Waded through a quagmire of regret. Not for his beliefs. Only the torrent of events beyond his control.

But this feeling was altogether different. The fight burned in his gut. The line between justice and vengeance blurred as a raging tide coursed through Nolan.

They must be stopped.

Starlight shimmered over Windy Holler as they entered the yard. In the breezeway, glowing with lantern light, Aynsley stood and waited.

Nolan jumped down. "Get Becca and Eleazar. He's hurt."

Hitching her skirts, Aynsley jogged to the kitchen. The next moment, Eleazar bounded from the steps to help Nolan ease Kirby to the ground. In the moonlight, silent tears gleamed on Kirby's face.

Eleazar scowled. "What'd those bad men do?"

"Plenty. Let's take it easy." Nolan supported Kirby on one

side while Eleazar held up the other. On the porch, the three women waited, shadows obscuring their faces.

Kirby gasped and his head dropped, his legs collapsing.

"He's fainted." Nolan shouldered the weight.

"I got 'im." Grunting, Eleazar scooped the injured man into his arms and clipped past the ladies.

Becca stood aside and held open the kitchen door. After Eleazar had lowered Kirby onto the chair, the ladies inspected him, but when Aynsley unwrapped his hands, the air evaporated from the room.

"Merciful heavens." Aynsley clutched her stomach.

"Them rascals outta be set on fire, every last one of 'em." Becca seethed.

Eleazar's dark eyes met hers, a warning in his quiet voice. "Becca."

"I mean it. We're all thinkin' it, but I ain't afraid to say it out loud."

"How horrendous." Catherine examined one of Kirby's hands. "There's no need to rouse him before we clean them. It's better this way."

While the ladies worked, cleaning and tending the wounds, Eleazar eased next to Nolan peering out of the window. "You reckon they're out there?"

"I doubt it. They've done their mischief for the night. They're likely bibbing their whiskey and laughing." He shifted away and fixed his attention on the others. "I feel the same as Becca."

"The Good Book says, 'Vengeance is Mine, I will repay, saith the Lord.' Ain't our job to repay evil with evil."

"We can't sit by and take it, either."

"Mr. Nolan, the right time will come."

"Mayhap this is the time."

From the chair, Kirby stirred. "No, it's not." The ladies' eyes widened as they paused their ministrations.

"How long have you been alert?" Catherine clipped a fresh bandage from a piece of cloth.

"A few minutes." Kirby flinched when Becca began wrapping one hand. "Nolan, they want you to confront them on their grounds, but don't do it. Catch them here. Eleazar's right."

Nolan suppressed a frustrated sigh. "I'm sorry you're caught up in our troubles."

"I'm not. Just sorry I wasn't more careful. I won't be much use to you. When I can see again, I'll help watch, at least."

"I'm obliged to you." Skimming the perimeter of the yard, Nolan saw no signs of movement. Satisfied, he approached the table.

As Aynsley bandaged Kirby's other hand, he bit down on his lower lip. Compassion extinguished some of the fire in Becca's eyes. "It's a good thing they didn't hold your hands to the stove much longer. You'll have a few scars, but I think you'll get the full use of them when they're mended. I'll use my special salve. It'll heal 'em quick and keep away infection."

"Thank you, Becca."

A grim smile curved her mouth. "It ain't all me. It's taking the three of us to patch you up."

"I'm beholden to y'all."

Aynsley glanced at Nolan. "You'll stay here, Mr. Kirby, as long as you need." Nolan met her stare with an approving nod.

"It'll be for a short spell, at least until I can see."

Setting his rifle in the corner, Nolan strode toward the door. "I'll set up a cot in the parlor."

CHAPTER TWENTY-SIX

Muffled whimpers radiated through the midnight, and Aynsley's eyes sprang open. Her heart sank. Zadie wriggled beneath the covers of her makeshift bed on the floor—a narrow cotton mattress from their childhood.

"Mama?"

Aynsley squelched the urge to cover her ears and nudged Catherine, who was sharing the bed until laundry day when they would strip Elnora's bed and wash the sheets.

"Zadie is crying."

Rubbing her eyes, Catherine sat up and listened. "Poor thing. These days are going to be hard." She shifted toward Aynsley, lowering her voice. "You need to go to her."

Dismay formed a lump in her throat. "No, I can't do that." She crimped the covers between her fingers. "She's distressed, and I'll make it worse."

"Zadie must learn to depend on you first. I'll get her if she refuses to go to you. No matter how long it takes, she must see you'll be the first one to reach her. The first one who cares for her." Catherine gripped Aynsley's fingers. "You must do this."

Catherine's touch hardly bolstered Aynsley's courage. Zadie's choking hiccup shattered the stillness. Dragging in a lungful of air, Aynsley shoved aside the covers and set her feet on the wide-planked floor. She struck a match and lit the lamp.

The halo of light drove the night farther into the corners. The sniffling ceased. Aynsley crept to the little bed, careful not to approach too closely.

Wide, glistening eyes peeped from under the edge of the thin quilt. Aynsley read the alarm rising in them. She summoned her calmest voice. "Zadie, honey, I'd like to help you. May I rock you for a while?"

"I want Mama." Two large tears welled and spilled over, nearly crushing Aynsley's composure.

She inched closer. "I know you do. Shall I hold you till you sleep? Then you won't feel so lonely."

"Nooooo!" Zadie whipped the quilt over her head.

Helpless, Aynsley cut a glance at Catherine and spread her hands in defeat.

"Try once more," Catherine whispered, nodding her head toward the quivering lump.

Aynsley ignored the knot in her stomach. "Please. I'm your friend." Her chest ached with the hardest words of all to say. Ever since childhood, she'd had trouble expressing the secret places of her heart, but she would try. For Zadie.

"I ... I love you, Zadie Charlotte." She stroked the blanket gently with her fingertips.

The child screamed, rolling sideways, the pitch hurtling Aynsley against the wall. Immediately, Catherine hopped from the bed and flew to Zadie's side.

Her composed voice brooked no nonsense. "Aynsley is trying to comfort you." With casual movements, Catherine pried the cover from Zadie's face and shushed her sobs. "There now."

She cradled Zadie in her arms and carried her to the rocking chair near the window. "Why did you scream like that? You scared Aynsley and me." She kissed Zadie's clammy forehead. "You're not to be naughty like that again. No matter how you feel, you may not scream at anyone."

A hiccup racked Zadie's chest. Brushing her tiptoes against the floor, Catherine nudged the chair into motion. "Aynsley, dear, return to bed. You did well."

But she didn't feel so well. Aynsley's wobbly legs moved to the bedside. Slumping onto the mattress, she reclined against her pillow and watched Catherine soothe her small cousin.

The slow dip and sway of the chair lulled Zadie's quiet sobs. Aynsley's spirit, however, tossed and tumbled on waves of despair.

Catherine's quiet voice spoke through the tumult. "Crying is often the easiest thing to do. When the tears get trapped somewhere between your heart and soul, it's the hardest to bear."

"How do you know?" The tortured question tripped over her lips.

Catherine's azure eyes dimmed. "I just do."

Aynsley tucked the covers under her chin, hungry for a warm embrace. "What has life been like for you, Catherine?"

"Lonely and unending."

"But why? Your letters always sounded cheerful and full of news. Had you no friends?"

"I had plenty." A sad smile tugged the corner of Catherine's mouth. "But folks can't fill every hour of the day."

Aynsley ventured further, braving to ask the one question on her mind ever since Catherine's arrival. "Why did you leave the holler?"

Tipping up her head and shrugging, Catherine stared at the ceiling. "I longed for a life outside, beyond the horizon. I craved adventure, and I thought I had a right to choose my lot."

"I know what you mean. At times, the urge to run consumed my being, but my love for this place anchored me."

"You're fortunate. You may thank Stewart for it. He wanted you to feel as he did for this land."

"I do, but I fear it's costing too much."

Catherine stroked Zadie's curls, coaxing the child's eyes closed. "The cost is worth it, believe me. If I could do everything over, I would've chosen this holler, come what may. Then, I wouldn't have missed so much. Missed knowing you."

Aynsley's breath caught in her throat. "You're here now, and there's still time."

"Precious time. One of God's gifts, so easily snatched from one's grasp." Catherine met Aynsley's perusal. "You have that gift with Zadie. The days and weeks will draw her closer to you. Don't give up. Her mama's words will wane in her mind."

"But never in mine."

"Ah, they will, with the Lord's help. And your capacity for love will overcome."

Aynsley averted her gaze to the wall. Did Catherine truly realize how inept she felt? When Zadie grew older and learned of Aynsley's condition, would she be disgusted?

The thought of winning the child's love only to lose to eventual hatred gnawed at Aynsley.

Was it worth the risk? The pitiful sorrow on Zadie's face begged for love.

She had no choice.

CHAPTER TWENTY-SEVEN

"And I thought ladies were supposed to be gentle." Kirby braced his back against the chair.

Nolan bridled rising anger as Kirby flinched while Catherine and Aynsley tended his hands. A chalky pallor circled Kirby's mouth and seeped into his cheeks.

"Where did you hear such a falsehood?" Catherine kept a light tone while cleansing the wounds.

A strained breath hissed through his teeth. "The memory escapes me." Raising his eyebrows, Kirby peeked through the swollen slits of his eyelids.

"Don't try to look, Mitchum. The less you see, the better," Catherine commanded, her matter-of-fact manner belying the grimace on her face.

"I'm a sorry sight."

"Time will change that." Aynsley readied the clean, fresh dressings. "So far, there's no sign of infection. You should heal very well."

"As long as you behave." Catherine rounded the kitchen table to clean Kirby's other hand.

"I've no choice."

"But I do." Nolan shoved himself up from the chair.

He caught Aynsley's concerned glance. Two days had passed since the attack, and things had been quiet. Far too much. Similar to waiting for a tornado to wipe out the farm and everyone on it. Pressure coiled around him and narrowed its grasp.

Kirby turned his head in the direction of Nolan's voice. "It's best to let 'em come to you. They want to draw you out."

"I'm not arguing that point." He scraped a hand across his jaw. "I've got to get help somehow. The three of them can wreak a lot of havoc against Eleazar and me."

"No one wants to provoke the Hoskins." Aynsley handed the bandages to Catherine.

"Daniel will help, and Jed will follow."

At the mention of Nolan's two younger brothers, both women gaped at him. Nolan frowned. "At eighteen and sixteen, they're old enough. They'll do what I ask."

"And go against your mother?" Aynsley narrowed her eyes. "She made it clear that you're no longer family."

Though true, the words thrust like a bayonet under his ribcage. Clamping his jaw shut, Nolan left the room, each footfall quicker than the last one. He clipped outdoors toward the pasture.

"Nolan, wait."

Pausing, he kept his gaze ahead while Aynsley jogged to catch up. She reached his side, worry etched on her brow. "You can't go there."

"I must."

"You forget I can shoot as well as you."

Whirling to face her, he gripped Aynsley's upper arms. "Not you. I won't have it."

Confusion and anger battled across her face as she tried to tug herself free. Her brown eyes widened in outrage when he tightened his fingers. She tossed her head. "Windy Holler is as much mine as yours."

"And you belong to me."

Aynsley gritted her teeth, her eyes glinting. "I'm not a possession, subject to your whims."

Releasing her arms, he pulled her against his chest and buried his face in her hair. "That's not what I meant. I don't want to lose you. I'll do whatever it takes to keep you and our family safe."

Her rigid muscles relaxed. Slowly, her arms circled his waist, and the side of her face nuzzled his chest. "I'm sorry. I've been accustomed to being son and daughter to Uncle Stewart these last few years."

Despite his tension, Nolan chuckled. "You're by no means my son or daughter."

Her embrace tightened. "I'm used to helping."

"And you always do, but I can't let you stand in harm's way." He caressed her hair. "They forced your uncle into a corner, and I can't let that happen again."

"Suppose your brothers refuse?"

"Then we'll make do. With God's help." He stroked her back, drawing her closer. "You mean more to me than life, Aynsley. I want us to come out of this trial. Together."

When he loosened his hold, he cupped her chin in his palm. Wonder brought a hesitant smile to her lovely face, reminding him of a sunrise after a storm.

"That's my prayer," she murmured.

"We've not had time to ourselves, but we'll talk soon." He swallowed hard, braving a chance. "We have things we need to say to each other, don't you think?"

Her breathless answer fanned his cheek. "Yes."

A seed of promise took root in Nolan's spirit. Mayhap they would understand each other at last. Whistling for Thunder, he tenderly rasped Aynsley's jaw with his knuckles and released her.

"I'd be willing." Daniel cut a sideways glance at Jed. "How 'bout you?"

For a second, Nolan held his breath while the sixteen-year-old scraped him with a probing stare, a piece of straw perched between his lips. Jed had been twelve when Nolan left home. His younger brother had been a crack shot even then.

Finally, Jed dipped his head, nodding slowly. "I'm willing."

A trickle of relief eased Nolan's angst. "I'm beholden to you both. Now, I have to convince Mother."

The young men raised their brows, their grimaces dubious. Daniel nodded toward the homeplace. "You'll not have long to wait. Yonder she comes."

Swirls of dust kicked up from Viola Borden's boots as she tromped across the furrows. Even from that distance, Nolan spied the glint in her blue eyes.

"Botheration." Jed puffed out a breath. "She's madder than a wet hen. She never lets us have any fun."

"Fighting the Hoskins ain't exactly fun," Nolan cautioned.

"Better than this here." Jed hurled a frown across the field.

Daniel crossed his arms. "He's got a bit of a wild streak. I haven't yet thumped it out of him."

"Men will likely be killed." The faint shrieks of other battles rattled through Nolan's mind.

"And it'll be a pleasure to let 'em have it." Jed punctuated his words by smacking a fist into his palm.

Nolan flattened his lips together. No use in talking sense to that one. Having never tasted the bitterness of a bloodbath, Jed missed the gravity of his own words. A heavy tension, thick as the humid air, descended around the brothers while their mother halted.

"I told you never to come back here."

"And I wouldn't have, but I'm not too proud to ask for help. The Hoskins are pressing us hard. They hurt Mitchum Kirby a few days ago—held his hands to the stovetop and burned them."

A flicker of unease rippled through Mother's eyes. "I hate to hear it, but he's a fool for sticking his nose in other folks' business."

"They're going to attack again. They burned Becca and Eleazar's cabin."

"They ought to move on."

Nolan stiffened. "We're going to see this through, one way or the other."

"One way or the other, it'll be without my boys."

"See here, Mother." Jed whisked the plow's strap over his head and shouldered through Nolan and Daniel.

Mother held up a hand. "No, you listen. Your pa was bushwhacked because your brother joined the Yankees, and I'll not stand by and let you join him."

"We're old enough to decide." Daniel's tone, though respectful, held quiet authority. "We can't let those men run our lives. It ain't gonna stop. Ever since they killed Stewart O'Brien, they've gotten mighty big for their britches. No one'll ever have peace in this valley if we don't stop them."

Tucking her chin, Mother bristled. "He made his bed, he can lay in it."

Nolan hardened himself against the hurt edging into him. She spoke as though he wasn't her flesh and blood. Her rejection smarted like a slap across his cheek.

Jed set his jaw. "I'm going with Nolan."

Curling her fingers into fists, Mother jammed her hands onto her hips. "You are? Then you'll burn your bridges here."

"So be it." Jed's chest expanded.

"No." Nolan clapped a hand on Jed's shoulder. "You'll stay here, and Daniel too. You can't leave Mother and this place unattended. She needs you more than I do."

"It ain't right, makin' us choose." Jerking the piece of straw from his teeth, Jed tossed it to the ground and stalked away, bursting a dirt clod with a swift kick.

Mother sucked in a seething breath, leveling her glare at Nolan. "You've got your gall, making trouble here."

Daniel stepped forward. "Mother—"

"Stop or you'll be taking your leave." Her stare never wavered from Nolan's. "Get off this place. You've chosen your lot, and I'll have no part in it. No son of mine would've taken that gal to wife."

Anger tremored through Nolan's fingers. The insult cut to the quick, slicing through his defenses like a new saber.

"And no mother of mine would be so cruel."

The quiet words banished the livid flush from Mother's cheeks. Tearing his gaze from hers, Nolan stalked toward his stallion and swung into the saddle.

The next instant, Thunder was galloping toward home.

CHAPTER TWENTY-EIGHT

"I didn't expect much different, but I had to at least try." Nolan set his coffee cup on the table, his glance encompassing everyone.

The afternoon and early evening heat had driven them to set the supper table in the breezeway. Aynsley dabbed her mouth with her apron. Across from her, Zadie sat on the bench between Catherine and Mr. Kirby. Unable to hold a spoon, he leaned closer to Catherine as she fed him a bite of potatoes. The swelling in his eyes had receded enough that he could at least see. Observing his injured face, splotched a purplish black almost the color of eggplant, Aynsley choked down a gag.

She set aside her fork. "It's because of me. I'm sorry, Nolan." Aynsley's eyes smarted.

"You owe no one an apology. Her grudge against me goes far deeper." Beside her, Nolan brushed her fingers with his, a featherlight touch in front of family.

"No one knows for sure who killed your step-father. It might be the very men who are after you." Kirby accepted another spoonful from Catherine.

The muscles in Nolan's cheek jumped. "The thought occurred to me."

"Tomorrow's the Lord's Day. Zeke's unlikely to start trouble then, him being such a good Christian." A sarcastic smile curled Mr. Kirby's lips, making him look ghoulish. Aynsley lifted a cup of water to her lips and focused on the crisp, clean taste.

Thoughts of Uncle Stewart hovered too near, the scenes of that devastating night as he lay dying in her arms pounded her temples.

Darlin', forgive me. One day—

She lowered the cup. "It won't end until they're all dead. Or us. Every one of us will have to fight."

"I'm handy with a gun." Catherine wiped a splotch of food from Zadie's chin.

Twisting half-way toward Aynsley, Nolan frowned. "We've already discussed this."

"Before you tried to enlist your brothers' help."

A stubborn cloud darkened his face as he stabbed a carrot on his plate. "It's out of the question."

"Don't you realize you're cornered?" Aynsley rubbed the tender skin of her temples. "We can't be bystanders."

"Aynsley." His quiet warning sparked like gunpowder across her nerves.

All eyes across the table fastened on them. Holding the spoon halfway to her mouth, Zadie paused, her bright stare ricocheting between Aynsley and Nolan.

Warmth tinged her neck and cheeks. Shoving herself and the chair away from the table, Aynsley stood, her voice equally low and charged. "If you think I'll stand aside and allow you to die in my arms like Uncle Stewart, then you're sorely mistaken." Against her will, a sob choked her remaining words.

Nolan's head snapped up, surprise registering on his face.

Blindly, she rushed from the table, her wobbly legs carrying her into the yard where she collapsed against the side of a tree. Tugging the handkerchief from her pocket, she buried her face into it while the tears flowed.

She despised herself for her weakness and lack of self-control, especially in front of Catherine and Mr. Kirby. However, the thought of losing Nolan crushed the air from her lungs.

"Comfort her, Father in Heaven." Catherine approached, her skirts rustling the grass. She pressed a hand against the small of Aynsley's back. "You'll make yourself ill."

She gulped. "When I remember Uncle Stewart ..." Her eyes overflowed afresh.

"I didn't know you held him." Catherine's voice roughened. "I'm sorry."

Aynsley captured a calming breath. "I can't talk much of it. He asked me to forgive him before he went. I wish I knew the reason."

"Shhh." Pulling the handkerchief from her fingers, Catherine dabbed Aynsley's eyes and cheeks. The soft strokes eased the torrent cascading over her.

She peeked through her puffy eyelids. Shock stemmed the flow when she saw the wet streaks dripping from Catherine's face.

Lowering the handkerchief, Catherine fingered one of the embroidered flowers in its corner. "The message of nobility and beauty in these flowers suits Stewart. He was noble and beautiful in his love and commitment to you. And your ways are like his." She traced the *S* and brought it to her lips.

The loving gesture quelled Aynsley's grief. A misty smile curved Catherine's mouth and shimmered in her blue eyes. "And here comes someone who can better allay your sorrow than I."

Laying the handkerchief in Aynsley's palm, Catherine

nodded toward Nolan waiting at a respectful distance. After a final squeeze of her hand, she took her leave toward the house.

"I didn't mean to sound harsh." Nolan circled Aynsley's waist with his hands and pulled her close.

"Neither did I." Nuzzling against his chest, Aynsley took refuge in his strength. "I didn't want you and Eleazar to fight alone."

"Let me think on it. All of us will have to be prepared." He stroked her neck, his hand kneading the tight muscles. "I wish I could hide you away 'til it's over."

"Will this never end? In the beginning, we thought we were safe from the fighting, but our people have been stripped of almost everything. When will it be enough?"

The steady thrum of his heartbeat vibrated against her cheek while he spoke. "I honestly don't know. All we can do is take each day as it comes."

How well Aynsley knew it.

Nolan's fingers drifted into the tresses at the nape of her neck. With a gentle tug, he tilted her face upward and searched her eyes. "Since the parson isn't on our circuit this week, we'd better stick close to home and do our devotions here. After that, how about a walk to the orchard, just you and me? I have some things I'd like to say."

The anxious, unsure gleam in his eyes spoke of longing and trepidation. Aynsley's pulse shuddered and thrilled all at once. And yet, she restrained herself from hoping too much. Once she laid bare her soul, how would he see her then?

She imagined the light dying in his loving gaze, smothered by the truth. Like a cold, empty hearth bereft of a blazing fire.

Aynsley closed her eyes and hid her face in the security of his embrace.

The hinges creaked as Aynsley opened the trunk in the privacy of the bedroom. The rusty squeak pierced the silence, and she instinctively glanced over her shoulder.

Across the landing, Catherine and Zadie shared the other bedroom for the first time since Elnora's passing. The freshly laundered covers had erased all trace of death.

Sitting motionless, Aynsley strained her ears for sounds of crying. Nothing had persuaded Zadie to stay with her. Though Zadie couldn't be blamed, her rebuff pricked places already sore.

No muffled sounds sifted through the walls. Relieved, she peered into the depths of the trunk and rummaged through the remnant of years. The spicy scent of cedar invaded her nose. An overpowering smell of past and present. She shoved aside several quilts and books. At the bottom, as far as she could bury them, lay the letters. Her fingertips brushed their corners.

She licked her lips and pulled out the bundle. "I must be honest, but Nolan has his own explaining to do as well."

Though she knew the contents, his handwriting beckoned her to open them. To release the hurt and shock afresh. She withdrew the pages from one envelope and squinted at the sentences. Her eyes stumbled over them as they had many times through the years, as she begged her mind to read the words.

Instead, the letters shimmied, evading comprehension. Sweat pebbled her forehead and dampened her back.

Though I hold you in the deepest regard, you will always be a dear sister to me. Aynsley could practically hear Nolan's voice. *Let us not spoil our friendship with impossible dreams.*

Aynsley gnashed her teeth. "Lord, I need to see these words—just once."

She stared harder at the page, and the words swam, dazing her senses. Her fingers itched to crumple the pages into her fist. The memory of Elnora's laughter pealed like ringing bells and shattered her remaining concentration.

Aynsley sprang to her feet, spilling the papers onto the floor. Stumbling to the window, she hoisted it up and leaned over the sill. She drew in the night air and harnessed her tumbling emotions.

Nothing, however, could tame her mental deformity.

CHAPTER TWENTY-NINE

In the darkness of the front porch, sleep weighed down Nolan's eyelids while he skimmed the tree line. Nervousness juddered through him. The unknown lurking in the shadows didn't shake him, though.

Aynsley unnerved him to his core. He'd done everything but confess his love for her. Surely, she must suspect it. Tonight, when he'd held her, Aynsley returned his embrace but hid herself in his arms. Why was she afraid? Part of him dreaded the answer. Had he misinterpreted her once again?

Yet, when he remembered her answering kiss, the truth vanquished all doubt.

The cool midnight air feathered over his heated face and neck. Curling his fingers around the barrel of the rifle across his lap, Nolan groaned. Would the Good Lord allow them time to discover the truth or would this present danger tear them apart forever? He had no desire to die in Aynsley's arms. Only to live.

"It's about time for you to catch some sleep. You look beat."

Nolan grunted while Kirby shuffled to the chair beside his. "You're tellin' me?"

His movements stiff, Kirby lowered himself onto the seat and let out a pained laugh. "I reckon I ought to know."

"I'd say so. Are you sure you can take a watch?"

"I can squeeze a trigger, if need be. At least I can finally see."

The familiar ache stabbed through Nolan's thigh, and he shifted in the chair, resisting the urge to rub it.

Kirby squinted. "The old wound acting up?"

"A bit. It doesn't like this night air." Unable to clearly see Kirby's face, Nolan felt his sympathy.

"Thank God the war is over, though we have hard times ahead. I pray we keep what you and others have purchased."

The pulsing chirps of crickets filled the gap of unsaid words between them. Likely, his war wound had saved his life that fateful day. Had he pushed farther, he would've died in the cornfields of Antietam. He'd purchased little compared to others.

Nolan dipped his head and shook it, cramming the sights and sounds to an unforgotten corner of his mind. Though men didn't speak of those horrors, they lived and breathed them thereafter 'til they ebbed and flowed with the pace of living. Like grief.

He shifted his thoughts. "I'd like to ask you about Catherine."

"And?"

"I appreciate everything she's done, but I'm curious about her loyalty to Stewart's memory."

"Curious or suspicious, Nolan?" Kirby leaned forward, perching his arms carefully on his knees. "I've caught you watching her. And me."

"Why would she drop her life in Missouri to come to Aynsley's aid? Simply because Stewart requested it?"

"She had nothing holding her there, and Stewart trusted

her implicitly. You must remember he wrote that letter, knowing Aynsley would be unprotected if he died." Kirby cocked his head. "He stipulated she marry or lose the farm because he knew the consequences if she remained vulnerable. Catherine was Stewart's way of buying time for Aynsley. She could shield her from a forced marriage to Tom Hoskins."

Unblinking, Nolan stared at Kirby's shadowed face. The astute lawyer nodded. "Catherine isn't after a piece of Windy Holler. But the Hoskins are. Tom's had his eyes on Aynsley for quite some time. So, you see, there's more than one reason they want Becca and Eleazar gone. A nice farm and a beautiful girl all for the taking. And you've come along and spoiled their plans."

Anger flashed like fire striking gunpowder, spurring Nolan from the chair. He locked his jaw as he gazed into the starry sky.

Behind him, Kirby stifled a moan. "It's Providence you came. I would've protected Aynsley myself, though I'm of no use at the moment."

"By marrying her?"

Kirby's sober answer brooked no nonsense. "Yes, but not for love. I'm old enough to be her father. And my heart belongs elsewhere."

"It's not easy to say, but I feel a bit foolish for distrusting you both." Nolan gestured to Kirby's hands. "After all, you're caught up in our troubles whether you like it or not."

Kirby shrugged. "I have my own debts to pay … to Stewart and Catherine. These hands will mend. The other things …" He bowed his head and fell silent.

Setting the rifle aside, Nolan braced his palms against the porch railing. "If we can make it through this."

"The future is ever elusive, no matter the circumstances."

Every fiber of Nolan prayed they would prevail. *How* was

in God's hands. The odds were against him without Kirby's skills. When it came to shooting, the Hoskins didn't miss.

Aynsley swallowed the dry lump in her throat and slid the three letters into her skirt's pocket. Snapping the trunk shut, she wished she could sever the anxiety the same way. Her chest deviated between heaviness and weightlessness.

After leaving her room, Aynsley paused outside Catherine's door and raised her hand to knock. She needed a word of encouragement, anything to bolster her confidence.

For a moment, she listened, but no sounds came from the room. Perhaps Catherine was napping. She'd mentioned having a bit of a headache at dinnertime. Aynsley lowered her hand and moved from the door.

Her footsteps dragged across the landing and down the stairs where Nolan waited in the breezeway. The click of a revolver's cylinder pricked her ears. Nolan pocketed the firearm, undoubtedly bringing it for their safety. Even a walk to the orchard might prove dangerous.

When he heard her, he sent a smile that melted her heart. He plucked up Longfellow's book of poems from the side table and held out his other hand to her.

Aynsley cracked an unsure smile and grasped it. He intertwined their fingers, warmth radiating between them.

"Are you ready?" The low timbre of his voice sent a shiver of delight and dread through her.

She managed a nod.

Slightly limping, Nolan led her from the breezeway into the backyard where Becca and Eleazar watched Zadie dance with her Maggie near the rosebush. Reclining in a chair under an oak, Mr. Kirby dozed, his chin bobbing against his chest's rhythmic rise and fall.

Though they spoke little on the path to the orchard, Aynsley felt more at home by Nolan's side than anywhere else. She peeked a sideways glance at him. The afternoon sun glinted off his sandy waves. His broad shoulders filled out a blue, freshly laundered shirt. Despite Nolan's long hours of work, the homecooked meals had smoothed the hollows of his cheekbones. Aynsley's eyes roved the bridge of his nose where she spotted the faint, remaining freckles from childhood.

Then, as now, she wondered what he saw in her.

Nolan squeezed her fingers tenderly as though he understood. His eyes twinkled as he caught her perusal. Aynsley's neck tingled. Her glance scurried along the path to the apple trees.

Overhead, the birdsong filled the branches like an explosion of colors disguised as music. Aynsley's heart danced. As they neared the orchard, she imagined the different hues of every note, facets of happiness.

Long ago, she'd confessed her imaginings to Elnora. Her appalled reaction had silenced Aynsley. Abruptly, she swiped away the daydream and sharpened her focus on the apple trees.

Into the orchard they ambled. The swaying grasses rippled like emerald waves between the rows of fruit trees laden with a future harvest. Aynsley admired the growing fruit, almost tasting the pies and cobblers they would make.

They would have to guard it well. During the last three years, soldiers, stragglers, and vagabonds from both sides had stripped the fruit, barely leaving anything behind.

Interrupting her musings, Nolan led her beneath the shade of one of the larger trees. "How about here?"

Aynsley nodded. "It's a lovely spot."

As his gaze snagged hers, Nolan pulled her a tad closer until her skirts swished against his ankles. Aynsley's breath evaporated under his bright, intense perusal. She bounced away her glance to the trees behind them.

"Where do we begin?" she stuttered.

"Together."

The book of poems dropped to the grass. Capturing her face between his hands, Nolan stepped closer and brushed his lips against her forehead. The tip of her nose. Her cheeks. Last of all, he sought her lips, his face hovering over hers. The space of a few rapid heartbeats passed while he waited for her protest, his blue eyes darkening.

Casting aside her doubts, Aynsley closed her eyes and rested her hands against his solid chest. Waiting.

Nolan took possession of her lips. For long moments, they became lost as the years floated away, and they discovered the wonder of home clasped in each other's arms.

A bit later, Nolan pulled slightly away, his breath shaky. "Mayhap we understand each other a bit better than we realize."

CHAPTER THIRTY

As Aynsley's eyelashes fluttered open, the confidence waned from her face. She scrutinized Nolan's expression. "What is happening between us?"

He gestured to the grass. "Would you sit with me?"

Nodding, she accepted his outstretched hand, and he helped her sit. Aynsley smoothed her rumpled skirts as he settled beside her. Her hands then flitted over her raven hair, securing and tucking the strands he'd inadvertently loosened.

A wicked smirk curved his mouth, and she smacked his shoulder. "Do you mind?"

"Actually, I do." For good measure, Nolan plucked out several hairpins. Her waves tumbled past her waist and skimmed the grass.

"Nolan Scottsdale!" she squeaked. "You're behaving like a naughty schoolboy."

Chuckling, he tunneled his fingers farther into Aynsley's silky tresses and wheedled out the rest. Her dusky flush heightened. "Well, I never."

From his palm, he spilled the pins beside the book of

poems and dusted his hands as though glad to be rid of the pesky things. "Me neither. I've wanted to do that for a long time."

His gaze meandered over her. Ah, but she was beautiful to behold. Her hair flowed free of its restraints, and she looked like a young girl, the war-weary years and sorrows erased from her face.

A curious glint lit her brown eyes. "How long?"

"Ever since you started wearing it up."

Surprised, she tilted her head. "That's quite a long time."

"Forever."

All playfulness fled as they stared at one another, unanswered questions wedging between them. Nolan's pulse thundered as a flood of emotions cascaded over her features.

Aynsley fumbled with the cuff of her sleeve. "What are you saying?"

"You can't pretend not to know."

A confused frown narrowed her eyes. "I'm not pretending, but I am baffled, especially after your ..." she pulled in a quavering breath, "...adamant letters."

"What do you mean?" Nolan sat up straighter.

Aynsley clamped her hands together. "You said, 'Though I hold you in the deepest regard, you will always be a dear sister to me. Let us not spoil our friendship with impossible dreams.' Your words. *Impossible*. Why did you change your mind?"

Shock exploded like a cannonball through Nolan. He blinked. "I never said any such thing."

"Don't tease me, Nolan."

"I'm in earnest. There's not an ounce of truth in those words."

"Are you saying I'm a liar?"

"Not a bit. You must have somehow misunderstood, though I don't see how. I was very clear."

"You most certainly were. And then you kiss me as if you—"

She bit her lip and yanked a bundle of letters from her pocket. She brandished them under his nose. "Do you deny you wrote these?"

Nolan took the letters and glanced over them. His handwriting. Dirt-stained and grimy from the battlefields, the outpouring of his soul seared his palm. He flinched as though an old wound had ripped open.

"No, I don't deny it." He tamped down his own flash of temper.

Aynsley crossed her arms, a silent challenge in her expression. Resisting the urge to rip into the envelope, Nolan withdrew the letter and unfolded the pages.

"Oh, yes. Here it is:

"My Aynsley, every mile tears me farther apart from you. I remember your tears when we said goodbye and regret not confessing my heart on the spot. I could not speak for fear you might not return my sentiments.

"Now, surrounded by strangers and alone, uncertain of the future, I am compelled to admit my feelings concerning you. Always, my heart yearns only for you. And it always shall. You have my undying devotion and my eternal love.

"I can no longer hide it. I love you with every breath I take, waking and sleeping. You possess a place in my soul that no one else ever could. Can I dare to believe you might feel the same? Would you wait for me to return?"

His voice tremored. He glanced up from the page to witness speechless disbelief shatter the anger from Aynsley's face. Her fingers fluttered around her throat.

Nolan opened the next letter, skimmed to the closing paragraph, and read it aloud.

"I am waiting for your answer. I pray my letter has not upset you. Mayhap I misinterpreted your face at times when we looked at one another. I would rather have your love than friendship; however, I would rather have your friendship than nothing at all. My darling girl, all I ask is a chance to win you. We are kindred souls. Allow me to make you the happiest woman in all the world."

This time, he studied her intently. The rapid rise and fall of her chest. The prickling of her dark, rounded eyes. Innocent and unaware, as though hearing the words for the first time.

The notion stunned him.

He unfolded the final letter, short and to the point. He'd penned it after receiving Aynsley's answer. As with the others, he began reading near the end.

"I will trouble you no further. It pains me to lose a friendship I counted as one of the best I have ever known. I pray you find happiness, Aynsley."

"Yes, I recognize that one!" She pointed to the page as though grappling for light.

Like one lost in a dark room.

Laying aside the letters beside the poetry book, Nolan surveyed Aynsley and took her hand. "Darlin', did you even read them?"

Choking on a gasp, Aynsley snatched away her hand and leaped to her feet. Gathering her skirts, she sprinted through the rows of trees. Her raven locks streamed behind her.

In several strides, Nolan caught her elbow and whirled her around to face him. She dipped her head, unwilling to meet his eyes, while tears gushed down her cheeks.

Nolan gathered her against his chest and pressed his lips

into her hair. Sobbing, Aynsley grasped two handfuls of his shirt and buried her forehead farther.

He cradled the back of her head in his palm. "Tell me, sweetheart."

"Oh, Nolan," she wailed, trembling. "I didn't read them. I can't."

"What do you mean?"

"I'm unable to read." A fresh storm of her tears soaked through the front of Nolan's shirt and into his spirit. His mind raced through the past, the times they'd spent together, the hours they'd read together in this very place. No, the times he'd read to her. He recalled the pure joy, the happiness on her face in those moments.

She'd never even hinted.

And then, he recalled Aynsley's letter. "Wait a moment." He released her and jogged over to the poetry book. Thumbing through the pages, he plucked out the envelope and returned to her, holding it out.

"Can you explain this?"

After dabbing her handkerchief against her eyes, Aynsley tentatively took it and examined it. "What is it?"

"It's a letter from you."

She shook her head, her words faint. "I didn't send a letter. Nor did I have anyone else write it."

Nolan retrieved it from her hand and opened it. He skipped the airy parts and paused at the bit that had sealed his heartbreak.

"Though I hold you in the deepest regard, I could never promise my heart."

Anguish pinched Aynsley's eyes closed. "I didn't utter such a thing. I never wrote those words."

"But someone else did." They had been duped. Itching to hit something, Nolan wadded the paper into a crumpled ball. A face rose in his mind. His head snapped toward the graveyard.

A horrified gasp shook Aynsley. "Elnora."

CHAPTER THIRTY-ONE

All the scenes with her cousin whirled in Aynsley's memory. She stood motionless while coals of fury poured over her, churning up an icy hatred she'd never experienced.

Elnora, I don't understand.

That's the one consolation I have.

Elnora's voice raced through her mind, the clarity of her words sharpening into focus. Her consolation had been Aynsley's desolation. The times she'd poured over Nolan's letters, struggling to comprehend them while Elnora watched. Never uttering one word of truth. Allowing Aynsley to flounder in a web of lies.

Where was the sense in it?

Nolan approached, his hands spread wide, palms upward. "Why did you believe her?"

"Not long before you left, we'd become almost like sisters again. She was so sweet to me, like old times. We talked and laughed. Shared secrets." Aynsley's head throbbed. "I thought we'd put all the old quarrels behind us. And then your first letter came."

His hands circled her waist, steadying her against the tide

of emotions while she continued. "I was excited and a bit shy to ask Aunt Eva to read it." Aynsley glanced up. "You see, I suspected you might harbor feelings for me too. Elnora offered, so we went to our room. She opened it and glanced over the pages first."

"You couldn't tell anything by her face?"

"Not one spark. Nothing. She read it without any hesitation." She dug her fingernails into the tender flesh of her palms. "And I believed every word. I'm a fool, Nolan."

"No, you're not." He wrapped her in his arms, his tone forceful. "You're pure, not willing to believe evil of those you love." Nolan kneaded her back, his hands firm and comforting. "Why did you never learn to read?"

Humiliation overtook Aynsley, but she had to face it. "I'm unable to comprehend the letters." Her ribcage quaked. "I have a mental deformity."

Nolan's eyebrows crashed nearly together. "What are you talking about?"

Breaking free of the fetters, her answer gushed from anguished depths. "When I see a word and try to read it, the letters jumble together, making no sense. No matter how hard I try to concentrate, it grows worse. As a child, I overheard Uncle Stewart and Aunt Eva discussing it. They worried about my mind. Wondered what was wrong, if it was a deformity of some sort."

The taut muscles in Nolan's forehead eased. "So that's why you closed your eyes when you signed your name. I noticed it when you signed our marriage license and the papers at the lawyer's office."

"Uncle taught me how to memorize the letters' strokes in my name. If I close my eyes, I can focus on the movement of my hand rather than the word." Aynsley's face crumpled. "So, do you see why I was afraid to show you how I feel? You married someone with a mental weakness. If we were to have children—"

She waited for the light in his eyes to fade. Instead, it burned brighter, melting all her fears like wax before a flame.

"Sweetheart, listen to me. I know beyond all doubt you have no mental deformity."

When she opened her mouth to protest, he touched a finger to her lips. "I daresay, though your uncle knew you well, I know you best of all. I had a man in my troop who had the same problem as you. He would get disoriented if he looked at a piece of paper and tried to decipher it. But he was the most intelligent man in the entire unit."

Aynsley's heart quieted. "He was?"

"He could memorize anything spoken, and he was a master at arithmetic. Very much like you."

Nolan's caresses released the heartache she'd carried for so long. For the first time, hope wedged through the barren places of her spirit.

Nolan tilted his head closer. "What a terrible burden you've borne alone. Tell me, did Elnora taunt you?"

Her silence was his answer. Instead, she fingered his collar, all the insults locked in a dark corner out of sight.

Nolan's blue eyes glinted. "We've been wounded by someone we'll never see this side of eternity. But we'll overcome it together."

Though she'd chosen to love her cousin rather than hate many times, all affection drowned in the storm of her anger.

Yet Elnora lay in the graveyard, unable to bear the brunt of it or wield more injury. Hatred would plague Aynsley worse, if she allowed it.

Her lips tremored. "How can I forgive such cruelty and deceit?"

"By God's hand. He's made it right, and He'll lead us

through the rest." Tipping her chin up, Nolan lowered his lips to hers.

For the first time, no secrets or doubts lurked between them as they savored their mutual love. Aynsley prayed nothing else would ever part them.

Shattering the tranquility of the orchard, gunshots sliced the air, punctuated by Zadie's scream.

Before she could react, Nolan thrust Aynsley and himself onto the ground. The force of the impact knocked out her breath.

"Are you all right?" he asked, hovering over her.

She nodded and snagged some air into her lungs. Nolan scanned the area and leaped to his feet, afterward hefting Aynsley to hers. He seized the pistol from his pocket. "Let's go. Stay behind me."

Keeping pace with his long strides, Aynsley strained her ears but heard nothing else. When they neared the yard, Nolan slowed his steps and paused, his glance darting across the open ground.

Sounds of weeping drifted on the air. Near the dogtrot, Becca crouched on the ground as Eleazar and Mr. Kirby stood over her. Catherine knelt and touched her shoulder.

"It looks clear. Come." Nolan sprinted toward them, keeping Aynsley close behind him.

"Them bad men rode up and took Zadie!" Becca wailed, rocking. "She was right here with me, 'an Ardy snatched her up on the horse."

Dragging a hand through his hair, Nolan pocketed the pistol. Panic seized Aynsley, rooting her feet to the ground.

Mr. Kirby shook his head as though dazed. "Zeke said they'd be waiting at Black Cavern and not to come until Becca and Eleazar are gone. Then they'd let Zadie go. They've set a trap for you, Nolan."

Catherine stood. "Tom struck Becca down with his rifle."

"I'm all right. I've been hurt worse in my time." Becca rubbed her jaw. Reaching down, Eleazar lifted her from the ground.

Nolan glanced toward the pasture where the horses grazed. "I'm going to follow and scout it out first. Make sure that's where they are. Then I'll double back and figure out what to do. Whatever it is, it'll be best to wait 'til nightfall."

Aynsley forced her leaden feet to move, latching onto Nolan's arm. "Be careful."

"I'll see you in a bit." He squeezed her hand and whistled for Thunder. "You'd best get your gun in the meantime."

Not daring to think too far ahead, Aynsley whispered a prayer for Zadie and scrambled to the upstairs landing. She burst into the bedroom, crossing to the dresser and tugging open the drawer. Underneath her folded stockings lay the Colt.

She hitched up her dress. Not long after the beginning of the war, Uncle Stewart had urged her to make a hidden pocket within the folds of her skirts—an unlikely place for a pistol to hide. Right below her knee, to the side, she'd sewed and fashioned a pocket inside the layers of material.

"Thank you, Uncle Stewart, for your advice," she whispered, remembering his words as she placed the gun into the secret spot.

Keep the muff pistol in your outer pocket. If someone ever takes it, you'll have the Colt. Use it wisely, only when the opportunity affords.

She straightened her skirts and checked the smaller pistol. Catching her reflection in the mirror, Aynsley scowled at her untamed tresses. No doubt they'd be in the way. She snatched a ribbon from the drawer and bound her hair.

Though she felt the weight of the revolver, her skirt gave no evidence of its presence. She closed her eyes.

"Father, grant us the wisdom to know how to rescue

Zadie. Keep all of us safe and direct our steps. Comfort this child, wherever she is."

Imagining Zadie's terror, Aynsley pressed a hand against her aching chest. If only she could help her. Once more, she rechecked the Colt. Satisfied, she stepped onto the landing. As she hurried for the stairs, a flash of red and white snagged her glance.

She slowed and pivoted. A handkerchief lay near Catherine's bedroom door. In the panic, she must have dropped it while hurrying from the room.

The breeze fluttered one of its corners, and Aynsley's breath hitched.

As though in a dream, she moved nearer. Stooping over, she lifted it. If she had lived a thousand lifetimes, Aynsley would've recognized it anywhere, though she'd never seen it.

In three corners, an embroidered red pansy bloomed. A crimson S emblazoned the fourth corner.

Uncle Stewart's handkerchief. The one buried with Mother.

Aynsley spread the cloth over her palm, her fingers trembling as she traced the stitching, her pulse racing. Why was it here? With Catherine? Indignation churned in her spirit. She had no right to it. Sara was dead.

Or was she?

The question splintered Aynsley's thoughts like a hurled stone shattering a darkened pane of glass at midnight.

Stunned, she touched the cloth to her lips and inhaled, recalling the private moments between herself and Catherine. Her devotion to Stewart and his wishes. How she shut herself away from neighbors at Elnora's funeral. Her thorough knowledge of Sara. Why?

I knew her as well as my own soul.

All of a sudden, Aynsley had never seen so clearly.

Catherine was Sara.

In that instant, Aynsley knew what she must do. As she descended the stairs, a blessed numbness engulfed her. When she reached the bottom, she paused and listened. The backyard was empty.

Voices hummed in the kitchen. Everyone was occupied, tending Becca. All the better. The side table caught her eyes. Aynsley deftly folded the handkerchief and placed it there with the *S* facing upward. Pausing on the back steps, she scanned the yard. Maggie sprawled facedown where Zadie had dropped her. Aynsley remembered Catherine's words.

No matter how long it takes, she must see you'll be the first one to reach her. The first one who cares for her.

Zadie needed her the way she had needed Sara. Someone to share her troubles and run to her defense.

Aynsley hurried to the doll and tucked it under her arm. Before anyone spotted her, she dashed toward the woods in the direction of the cavern.

CHAPTER THIRTY-TWO

Casting long shadows from the house, the sun sank lower in the west as Nolan reined in Thunder at the farm. As he sprang down from the saddle, Catherine tore across the yard, her face pallid.

"Aynsley's gone to the cavern!"

Distress kicked him in the gut, spurring him toward the breezeway where Kirby and Eleazar stood. "Why didn't you stop her?"

"She slipped out." Kirby cut a glance at Eleazar. "Must have been while Catherine was helping Becca. We were in the kitchen."

"She'd gone upstairs. When we came out, we couldn't find her anywhere." Catherine clenched her hands together. "She took Maggie. It's the only place we could think of."

Becca buried her face in her apron.

A lump knotted in Nolan's throat. Growling, he smacked the wall with his palm, the muscles in his neck cramping at the impact. "Let me think."

His mind roared. *Father, grant me wisdom.* The plan he'd

formed on the ride home dissipated. Straightening, he paced to the back porch. *Show me, I plead.*

His stare fell on the side table where a cloth lay. The crimson *S* cried out to him, carrying him to other times when Aynsley had told him an old story. "What's this?"

Catherine fumbled with her sleeve. "Oh no. I had only just taken it out before the trouble started. Aynsley must have found it and left it there."

Snatching it up, Nolan whipped open the cloth. Red pansies. He squinted hard at Catherine. "What are you doing with Stewart's handkerchief? The one buried with Sara?"

Tears welled in Catherine's blue eyes. "I am Sara."

Disbelief knocked him back a few steps.

"She's telling the truth." Kirby neared, standing by Catherine's side.

"Then why didn't you tell us?"

Kirby winced as though the question slapped him. "It wasn't my business to tell."

Nolan wrangled the questions to a corner of his mind. "I can't think of that now. I need to figure out a way to get Aynsley and Zadie."

"You've got to go persuade your brothers somehow." Kirby pointed his bandaged hand in the direction of the Borden place.

"No such luck there. Mother might shoot me before the Hoskins can do it."

Catherine caught Nolan's sleeve. "Let me ride with you. I'll persuade her."

The intense look on her face gave him pause as he considered the idea. "I don't think it'll work."

"It's the only chance you have, Nolan. It won't hurt to try."

Expelling a pent-up breath, Nolan tucked the handkerchief into her palm. "All right. Eleazar, will you help me saddle another horse?"

"Yes, and I'll go along." Eleazar snatched his hat from a peg.

"You'd best stay here. It won't go well if the Hoskins catch you."

Halting, Eleazar pierced him with a fierce glance. "No one strikes my wife, Mr. Nolan."

How well he understood the feeling. Nolan nodded, falling into step next to him. "You're right. I'll be glad for the help."

Merciful Lord, prepare the way before us.

Pebbles and dirt crackled downhill as Aynsley treaded up the path to the cavern. Tall trees shrouded the area like silent sentinels, warning passersby to beware. The air grew thicker and more hushed with each step she took. Almost tangible.

A stick snapped beneath her boot, loud in the heavy atmosphere. She hesitated, her eyes closing. Sure enough, at the mouth of the cavern, scrambling sounds echoed.

"Come no farther lest you get a gut full o' lead."

Aynsley gulped and steeled her voice. "I've come to be with Zadie."

After a moment's pause, Zeke answered her. "I warn't born yesterday. You figuring to set a trap for us?"

In a way, yes. "Lord, forgive me," she muttered before raising her tone. "I'm here alone. No one has followed me. I'd like to make sure Zadie stays safe."

"Your husband knows where you are?"

"Not yet, but he will."

The men guffawed, the harsh, ugly sound grating along Aynsley's spine. "You're trying my patience, gal. If you be lying, I'll kill you."

"I'm not a fool. Might I come?"

"She's bold as brass, for sure." The smirk in Tom's voice sickened her. "Let her come up. I'll keep an eye on her."

While Zeke wavered, the idea chilled Aynsley all over like hoarfrost.

"Git on up, but take care if you want to get out of this alive."

The cavern's black mouth yawned in front of Aynsley as she drew closer. Zeke held up a hand. "Hold it. Tom, check her for weapons."

Shoving himself from his perch on a stone, Tom swaggered toward Aynsley, his gray eyes glittering. When his stare fell on the doll, he laughed, snagged it, and flung Maggie aside.

"Running away from home, girlie?" Towering over her, he seized her close. His rough hands scrubbed her person. Biting down a gag at the odor of sweat and filth, Aynsley held her breath.

He jammed his hand into her pocket and found the small pistol. "Well, lookie here, Zeke." He tossed it to his brother, who caught it in one smooth motion.

Spitting a stream of tobacco, Zeke inspected the firearm and scowled. "Never trust a woman."

Ardy chuckled from the shadows.

Yanking her closer, Tom continued his search.

"You beast!" Aynsley recoiled and kicked Tom's shin, full force. Rage flared his nostrils. His fingers clamped around her arms.

"That'll do." Zeke's quiet command released her from Tom's iron grip. She stumbled sideways, willing the hot moisture in her eyes to dry.

Tom glowered. "Next time, you won't be so lucky."

The weight of the Colt reminded Aynsley to maintain her composure the way Uncle had trained her. She snapped her jaw shut.

A bullet plopped onto the ground as Zeke unloaded her pistol. "You're a plucky one, I'll give ya that. Here." He dropped the weapon into Aynsley's hand. "It'll do you no good."

Not one hint of a sneer rippled over her face. A sock containing those very bullets were sewn within the other side of her skirts. She shoved the gun into its place.

Zeke raked a gaze over her as though trying to decipher her thoughts. Her glare clashed into his, shuttering her secrets.

Finally, he motioned for her to follow. "This way."

Ignoring Tom and Ardy, she retrieved Maggie and dusted her off as she walked to the cavern's mouth.

Moist, chilly air wafted over Aynsley when she stepped into the dimly lit cave. Shadows dangled from the rotund ceiling, lolling along the walls with the flicker of a flame.

Aynsley rounded an outcropping. A beam of light poured from a lantern sitting on a stone to one side. Several feet from it, Zadie sat like a tiny statue on the ground.

"Well, there she is. Not a hair of her head harmed." Zeke's gravelly voice lowered. "See it stays that-a-way." Sharpening his glare, he patted his sidearm and stalked outside.

Oval eyes fastened on Aynsley. Zadie's eyebrows arched over her swollen eyelids, the one part of her body that dared move. Dry tear trails streaked the smudges on her face.

Aynsley ventured a few steps and held out Maggie. "She was wanting her mama, so I brought her as quickly as I could."

Zadie darted a stare from Maggie to her.

Gathering courage, Aynsley lowered Maggie onto Zadie's lap. Cautiously, she backed away while the girl's gaze followed her.

"I'll be here every step of the way, Zadie Charlotte. Everything is going to be all right. Jesus will help us." She settled on the floor of the cave and spread her skirts around her legs, ensuring the Colt lay flat.

Half-sobbing, the child cradled Maggie and hid her face in the doll's neck.

Boots clomped into the space, and Aynsley looked up into Tom's predatorial scrutiny. The flesh of her arms pebbled. One side of his mouth quirked up, leering, as he lowered himself onto a large outcropping. Relaxing against the wall, he laid a pistol on his lap and crossed his arms.

Aynsley wrenched away her stare to Zadie. Somewhere, farther in the cavern, the trickling of water burbled. Resisting the urge to flex her fingers, she folded her hands in her lap. The revolver's cold, metal barrel rested beneath her leg.

Use it wisely, only when the opportunity affords.

CHAPTER THIRTY-THREE

Ol' Hickory bawled from beneath the porch as their horses approached the Bordens' split rail fence. A sapphire twilight cocooned the mountains and valleys through a veil of starlight. Far too serene for this troubled evening. Lightning bugs flickered within the pooled shadows of the trees.

The front door swung open and banged against the wall. As expected, Mother tramped across the threshold, shotgun in hand.

"You're trying my patience, Nolan. You've got gall, showing up after my last warning."

Before he could answer, Catherine urged her mare closer. "Viola."

Mother's hands slackened around the weapon, and she lowered it. Squinting through the dim, she descended the steps. "Who are you?"

"I'm Sara."

The gun slid from Mother's hands, but she snatched it up before it hit the ground. "No. Sara's dead."

"I was for a long time, but I've come home."

As Mother neared the fence, she surveyed Catherine for a

speechless minute, the moonlight casting an eerie sheen over her pale face. "It *is* you. How is it possible?"

"There's no time to explain. We need your help. The Hoskins have kidnapped my niece, Zadie, and we're sure they also have Aynsley at Black Cavern."

A glimmer of sympathy flitted through Mother's eyes before they hardened like granite. "That ain't my problem."

Catherine bent forward over the saddle horn. "There's an innocent four-year-old child trapped up there as well as my daughter. Nolan and Eleazar can't confront those men alone. They'll likely be killed."

Mother's glower burned into Nolan. "How dare you involve Sara, of all people, to ask my help."

"He didn't involve me. I insisted."

"You want a lot of me." Mother's chest swelled as she drew an indignant breath. "More than I'm willing to give. Tell me one good reason I should help you."

Catherine bent her head, her answer quiet. "There's none. I merely ask you extend grace to Nolan and Aynsley. They didn't wrong you. I sinned against God, against my family, and against you—my dearest friend. I've never ceased being sorry. Please, Viola, it's not for me. Don't punish them for my sins."

Mother recoiled as though slapped. Her gaze traveled beyond them, drifting toward the sky. Long seconds ticked while she searched its fathomless depths before dipping her stare at them.

"Daniel! Jed!"

The brothers popped into the doorway so quickly that, under other circumstances, Nolan might have grinned. Must have been standing out of sight, listening.

"The Hoskins are holding a little gal and Aynsley captive at Black Cavern. Are y'all willing to help Nolan?"

Daniel nodded while Jed smacked his hands together. "Right away."

Squaring her shoulders, Mother tucked the shotgun under her arm. "I'll come along. In a pinch, I daresay I'm a better shot than any of you."

By the time the group passed Windy Holler, the full moon silvered the hills. When they reached the house, Catherine chose to stay and help Kirby watch the place.

On the way, a plan developed in Nolan's mind, and they discussed the details. He would approach the cavern unarmed, but not until everyone else was in position.

The rest of the way, he prayed.

Bringing up the rear, Mother hadn't spoken since leaving the house. She'd listened to their plans without protest. Empathy erased his resentment. No telling the things she had endured those years he was absent.

The woods blackened the final quarter mile to the cave. Dismounting, they led the horses off the path and tied them.

"It'd be a mite easier if the moon wasn't full," Jed muttered, rechecking his rifle and strapping it over his shoulder. "Leastways, the trees will give us some cover."

Everyone except Nolan removed their shoes. They followed him, hardly making a sound. The heavy, night air swallowed most of it. Staying in the shadows, they picked their way up the trail.

Deeper into the woods, an owl screeched, raising the hairs on Nolan's neck. When they were in sight of the cavern, they stopped and surveyed the area. The silhouettes of two men stood near the opening where a huge stone shielded them in case of a shootout.

Nolan, however, prayed his plan would make the rock a

futile place to hide. He motioned to Jed and Eleazar. They leaned in, alert. "Those are the two trees yonder we talked about. Twenty-five yards from the cave's mouth. Think you can climb them?"

Jed nodded. "All I need is a boost off Daniel's shoulders, and I can climb high enough to get a clear shot."

"Don't shoot unless you must, Jed. You can't take back a bullet."

"I won't, but if they so much as raise a gun at you, I'll stop 'em."

Crouching silently near a bush, Nolan and Mother waited as the men maneuvered toward the trees, heading first to Jed's position. Climbing atop Daniel's shoulders, Jed stepped onto a branch, his bare feet gripping the tree's bark.

Next, Eleazar and Daniel angled across the slope, hunched in the shadows, their pace deliberate and slow until they arrived at the other tree. In the same manner as Jed, Daniel boosted Eleazar into the branches.

One of the Hoskins edged a step in their direction. He craned his neck. Had he heard something? From his build and height, it was likely Ardy. Holding his gun, he crept nearer the tree Eleazar had climbed.

Mother glanced at Nolan. They could do nothing but remain in their position.

From the cavern, Zeke spoke.

"You see anything?"

"Naw. Not yet."

Nolan held his breath and tried to make himself small. Closer Ardy slunk, pebbles crunching under his boots when he stopped within two feet of the tree.

Daniel, stay where you are.

Save for the sounds of the forest, no other noise seemed to alert Ardy to their presence. He pivoted slowly, scanning the landscape, and then headed to the cavern.

A relieved breath passed between Mother's lips. After a few minutes, Daniel emerged from behind another tree. Though he said nothing, his sober expression said everything when he met Nolan's eyes.

They couldn't afford for that to happen again.

The three of them blended farther into the dark cover of the trees. Nolan gestured to a huge stone roughly twenty-five feet from the cavern's entrance. "There's where you both will position yourselves. You'll flank them if they try to make a run for it. Remember, they won't be expecting me to have help. I'll give you time to get there."

Before they moved, Mother clutched Nolan's arm. "Watch your business."

"I'll do my best."

Ignoring the hammering of his heart, Nolan waited until he was sure they'd made it to the stone. Then, he stepped into the path.

He raised his voice. "Zeke Hoskin."

The two men jerked upright. "Be that you, Nolan?" Zeke's gruff voice barked.

"Yep. I'd like to have a word with you. Might I come up?"

"Come easy-like or you'll die where you stand."

I'm in Your hands, Father.

"Sounds like your no-good Yankee husband has come at last," Tom sneered, twisting his head at the sound of voices. He stood and spit near Aynsley's feet. "Took 'im long enough. It'll be a pleasure making you a widow."

He sauntered to the cave's mouth and stepped outside.

Sweeping up her skirts, Aynsley plunged her trembling fingers into the folds and seized the Colt out of its pocket.

A tiny gasp escaped Zadie's lips.

Peeking over Maggie's head, her stare latched onto the gun. Aynsley shook her head slightly and pressed a finger to her lips, wordlessly begging the child to obey.

Zadie buried her face in Maggie's yarn hair.

Somewhat relieved, Aynsley straightened her legs and swept a hand over her dress, smoothing it into place. While her eyes strained to watch the scene outside, she edged the revolver partly beneath her thigh and spread her skirt over the rest of it.

Now to wait for her opportunity.

"That's far enough," Zeke commanded. The three brothers faced Nolan, glowering. The moonlight skimmed their features, nearly as plain as daylight. At least he'd chosen Jed's and Eleazar's positions well. They'd have no trouble aiming.

Nolan halted. "Are Aynsley and Zadie safe?"

"Safe enough."

The men searched him for any sign of a weapon while Nolan held his arms motionless. Seeming satisfied, Zeke relaxed his stance a fraction. "I left word not to come unless your hired help was gone. Are they?"

"Why don't you come to the house and find out?"

Zeke scoffed, stroking his beard. "You'd like that, wouldn't you? Them gals won't leave this place until you do as I say."

"It's up to Eleazar and Becca. They're free to stay or free to leave."

Bristling, Zeke pointed a thick finger. "You're mighty foolish, coming here. And that wife of yourn is a bold one, walking up here in the midst of us demanding to see that girl. Shame she married a blue belly."

The insult did nothing to ruffle Nolan's composure, and Zeke tilted his head, squinting. "I can remedy that. Tom's had his eye on her for quite a spell. He'd teach her to learn her place."

"I'd like nothin' better." Tom flexed his hands, his dagger-like stare sharpening.

Ignoring him, Nolan kept his voice even. "I'm here to warn you. If you don't let them go, there's going to be bloodshed."

"Yep. Yours." Their obnoxious laughter hooted down the hillside, but Zeke's flinty gaze never wavered from Nolan's. "Your pappy tweren't such an easy kill as you. Caught 'im in the pasture alone, but, boy, did he put up a fight."

Grieved rage seared through Nolan's chest as he clenched his fists, but thoughts of Aynsley and Zadie anchored him.

"He died like a dog, though," Ardy growled. "Like you're fixin' to." Moonlight ricocheted from the barrel of his pistol.

A single gunshot split the air, and Ardy collapsed onto the ground. Dead. The stunned brothers froze for an instant before Zeke lunged at Nolan.

"No, Lord, let it not be Nolan." Aynsley moaned, her hand pressing against her mouth.

Tom stumbled around the corner and charged her, seething. "Ardy's dead!"

Aynsley jammed her hand beneath the skirt.

He yanked her upright, the jolt dislodging the Colt from her grasp. The revolver struck the ground.

Tom's fingers dug into the tender flesh of her neck. Aynsley wheezed, clawing his hands.

His sour breath blasted across her face. "He's dead. And you're gonna pay." His grip closed around her throat. Snarling, he shook her.

Aynsley's knees buckled with the intense pain.

Just as suddenly, Tom yelped and released her. He whipped

around. Zadie stood behind him. "You little hussy, biting me," he roared, backhanding her across the face.

Shrieking, Zadie toppled.

Aynsley dove for the revolver and grasped it. Taking aim, she clicked the hammer into place. Tom whirled toward her. From outside, the scuffling sounds of a struggle invaded the cavern.

Her pulse thrummed like waters racing toward a fall.

Tom sneered. "You ain't got the guts." He angled a step closer.

"Get away, Zadie!"

Crying, the child scrambled toward the cave's mouth but halted at the entrance and crouched low. Could she see fighting outside?

"Stop, Tom, or I'll shoot."

A murderous gleam lit Tom's dark eyes. He crept closer. "Then you'd better make it good, or I'll come for you wherever you are."

"That's far enough."

Tom paused, his stare deviating between her and the gun. "You can't get rid of me that easy." He sprang forward.

Aynsley squeezed the trigger.

CHAPTER THIRTY-FOUR

Zeke slammed into Nolan, and the two of them toppled to the ground. From the corner of his eye, Nolan saw Daniel and Mother approaching, their weapons drawn, waiting for a clear shot. Zeke's fist crashed into his jaw. Black spots exploded in his vision.

Gunfire rumbled and erupted from the cavern, spilling across Nolan and Zeke as they struggled. Summoning all his strength, Nolan knocked Zeke sideways, rolling him off his body.

As Nolan leaped to his feet, Zeke snatched a sidearm from his holster. The next instant, a shot cracked from Eleazar's perch before anyone else could react.

Zeke slumped onto the grass.

While Mother and Daniel scrambled to check the man, Nolan swiped Daniel's gun and darted to the cave, certain he'd find Aynsley lying in a pool of blood. His veins thundered. Tom would pay dearly. He rounded the corner, ready to confront his wife's murderer.

Instead, he burst inside to find Tom had already paid.

Astonished, Nolan lowered the gun. Aynsley stood over

Tom's body, her limp fingers holding a Colt at her side. She blinked, choking on a breath. "Nolan. Thank God." She pocketed the weapon within her skirts.

Rushing to Zadie's side, Aynsley scooped her into her arms. "Zadie Charlotte, everything is all right. You're safe." Whimpering, the child locked her fingers around Aynsley's neck and clung to her. Nolan slid the weapon behind his waist band and gathered them close, stroking Aynsley's hair as Zadie nestled between them.

"Praise God, you're both safe. I was sure Tom had …" Nolan shuddered and pressed his lips against Aynsley's forehead.

Aynsley sniffed. "He tried. I owe Uncle Stewart my life. And Zadie."

Though Nolan didn't know what she meant, he knew she'd explain later. He breathed in the scent of her hair, inwardly praising the Lord for their safety.

Aynsley's eyes widened as she inspected him. "Your jaw and eye, Nolan. You're hurt."

"As long as my girls are well, I'm all right. I'll heal."

Footsteps jogged toward the entrance. When Jed and Eleazar found them huddled together, they sputtered their relief.

"We didn't know what we were gonna find." Eleazar puffed, staring at Tom's body.

A white border fringed Jed's lips. Perhaps he'd learned a sobering lesson in bloodshed.

He dragged a sleeve across the sweat beading his forehead. "Zeke is alive. Shot through the shoulder, but I reckon he'll live. The bullet went clean through."

Nolan nodded. "Thank you both. Y'all saved my life."

Sidestepping Tom, Eleazar retrieved Maggie and tucked her in the nook of Aynsley's arm. "Zeke figures I shot 'im. He saw me jump down from the tree. He's raving mad."

Nolan grimaced. "I wish you'd stayed hidden, my friend."

"I'm a man, Mr. Nolan."

The simple truth said more than anything else. Gripping Eleazar's muscled forearm, Nolan blinked away the moisture rushing to his eyes.

While Jed yelled to Mother and Daniel that everyone was safe, Nolan ushered Aynsley outside. Zeke remained sprawled on the grass, probably weakened from loss of blood.

"We'll have to put them on their horses and take them to their place." Nolan dreaded the task. Zeke was the only one of the brothers who were married. Their elder parents also had a house on the property. He gritted his teeth against the nausea roiling in his stomach.

Eleazar kept his voice low. "I'll take the womenfolk home."

"I'm obliged. Jed, go along and fetch our horses." Nolan stroked Aynsley's cheek and buoyed himself for the unpleasant task at hand.

Disbelief rendered Aynsley speechless when she recognized Viola Borden in the darkness. The moonlight highlighted the premature threads of silver at Mrs. Borden's temples but erased the crow's feet around her eyes. For several seconds, they surveyed each other.

When they fell in step behind Eleazar and Jed, Aynsley sensed the woman's hesitation. The narrow path downhill forced them closer together than Aynsley wished. For a long while, the occasional skittering pebble was the only sound between them.

Though Mrs. Borden had hardened her heart against them, surely a sliver of love for Nolan remained secluded within her soul. Else, why would she have come? Her fiery words from that day in the churchyard had never ceased smoldering, searing a trail of guilt across Aynsley's conscience.

And Sara's return had compounded it. If she indeed was alive.

"Have you known, all this time, your mother lived?" Mrs. Borden's grim voice seemed to echo Aynsley's thoughts.

Aynsley's stomach plummeted. To hear the truth confirmed aloud bruised her spirit. Moments passed while she grappled for an answer. "No, ma'am. I'd been raised to believe she was my cousin Catherine. Uncle Stewart requested her return upon his death."

"I didn't know it either. Quite a blow for you, I'm certain."

"Considering everything that's happened, I haven't had time to think much on it." The look on Tom's face as he lay dying haunted her. She'd never seen raw fear like that. She blinked the scene from the forefront of her thoughts.

"I came because Sara asked me."

Aynsley skidded to a halt. "She asked you?"

Staring off in the distance, Mrs. Borden crossed her arms. "She did. Rode right up to the house and pled her case. I thought a phantom had come on horseback. Don't get me wrong, I ain't sayin' I'm ready to forgive. But she gave me some things to think on."

The two continued onward, matching the men's brisk strides. Aynsley shifted Zadie to her other hip. Since leaving the cavern, the child hadn't made a sound or moved. Her fingers remained linked around Aynsley's neck.

Mrs. Borden sighed wearily. "You're the image of your father."

"No one has ever told me." Aynsley chewed her bottom lip.

"Lookin' at you is almost like seeing him, especially the hair and eyes."

Aynsley's throat cramped. She hunted for the right words but found nothing. Apologizing for something she couldn't control was out of the question, and she'd suffered Mrs. Borden's tongue enough through the years.

They continued the rest of the way in silence, the emotions taut between them. Aynsley's thoughts drifted to Catherine. How could she face her? What would she say?

When they reached the horses, Jed mounted and led two of them toward the cave where his brothers waited. As his form blended into the darkness, Aynsley welcomed the gratefulness welling up. God had provided deliverance for all of them. While Eleazar readied his horse for her, she faced Mrs. Borden.

"If you hadn't allowed your sons to come, all of us might have been killed. Thank you, Mrs. Borden."

An abashed expression crossed the face of Nolan's mother. She fumbled loose the horse's reins from a branch. "Well, I figure blood is thicker than the past. What's between Sara and me has nothin' to do with you and Nolan." She set her foot in the stirrup and swung into the saddle. "I'd forgotten that."

If that was her apology, Aynsley accepted it. An admission of wrongdoing from Mrs. Borden was nothing short of a miracle. Bending down, Aynsley set Zadie on her feet. "After I mount, Eleazar will lift you up." She stroked the child's grimy head. "You were a brave girl tonight. You saved my life."

But the girl clutched Aynsley's neck tighter, mumbling incoherent words.

"What is it, Zadie?" Surely, she wasn't going to pitch a fit over riding a horse.

Her voice, shy and hesitant, fluttered at Aynsley's ear. "I … love … you."

"Oh, honey," Aynsley enveloped her in a hug. Her trek into the jaws of danger had been worth it. "I love you, too." She kissed Zadie's curls.

After releasing her, Aynsley mounted Eleazar's horse.

"All right, youngin', let's get you settled next." Eleazar's strong arms set the child in front of Aynsley. Zadie inspected her doll and smoothed its dress. "Thank you, Mister Ele'zar."

Aynsley circled an arm around her. "Time to go home."

"Thank the Lord you're both safe."

Heart in her throat, Aynsley skittered her gaze away from Catherine's tear-filled eyes. Lantern light from both sides of the dogtrot spilled onto the steps, lighting her path. Beside Catherine stood Mr. Kirby, relief flooding color into his face as she carried Zadie onto the porch. Becca clapped her hands together.

The clipping of horses' hooves underscored the uneasy throb of her conscience as Eleazar accompanied Mrs. Borden home.

"Everyone is safe. It didn't go so well for Tom and Ardy, though. Zeke alone survived." The words tasted acrid and unnatural on Aynsley's tongue, as though someone else had spoken them.

Becca exchanged a glance with Catherine and reached for Zadie. "I see you and our little one finally got acquainted. Here, child. Why don't I get you cleaned up and ready for bed, then Miss Aynsley will come say goodnight."

"Yes, ma'am." After a final squeeze, Zadie leaned over into Becca's waiting arms. Crooning in her ear, Becca headed upstairs, the comforting sound of her voice washing over Aynsley.

Her arms dangled at her sides, feeling strangely empty. Unable to meet Catherine's and Mr. Kirby's gazes, she emptied her pockets of the firearms, laying them on the side table. The handkerchief was gone.

She stared at the empty spot and expelled a breath. "I

killed Tom." Would the weight of the deed ever depart from her soul?

"Oh, Aynsley." Catherine's agonized voice came from close behind her. "I'm sure you had no choice."

"I didn't, but it makes no difference in how I feel."

"Unfortunately, I can't tell you how to feel, but time will help."

"Will it?" The burden of the entire day crushed Aynsley nearly to the breaking point. Like a dam straining under pressure. She spun around. "Are you truly Sara? My mother?"

Catherine's face blanched. "I am."

Aynsley's lips quaked, the anxiety brimming. "I should've realized."

"No, how could you have known it?" Sorrow crumpled Catherine's expression as she held out a hand.

"Indeed. How?" Aynsley stumbled blindly from her mother's reach. "I need to tend to Zadie."

The upstairs landing had never seemed so far away.

CHAPTER THIRTY-FIVE

The hushed swish of the bedroom door invaded the tumult of Aynsley's mind. Through the dim of the wee hours, she watched Nolan slip into the room and move toward the washstand.

Water poured into the basin. While he washed up, Aynsley stared at the ceiling and waited, the swishing of the water and Zadie's soft, steady breaths soothing her.

After rocking Zadie to sleep, she had scoured the grime and dirt from herself and collapsed into bed, hoping her tears would equally scour her soul.

After patting dry, Nolan rummaged in a drawer and donned his nightshirt. He crept to Zadie's makeshift bed, glanced over her, and tugged the cover a bit higher. His care for the child struck Aynsley to the core, love for him spreading into every corner of her heart.

"I'm awake."

Nolan hesitated, mid-step, on his way to the pallet. "How are you?"

"Not well," she admitted. "Will you hold me for a while?"

He didn't have to be asked twice. The bed sagged as he slid

next to her, clasping her against his broad chest. "I'm sorry, honey." He caressed her hair.

"Did you have trouble when you took them home?"

His muscles grew rigid. "Trouble enough. I warned Zeke never to return to the holler. He won't be so fortunate next time."

"He won't listen."

"He's used to his brothers doing his dirty work. It's a good thing he's not well-liked in these parts."

Aynsley shuddered. "What is wrong with me, Nolan? Part of me wishes he'd died too. Am I so callous?"

"No. After living through battle, I've felt it. You dread a future fight and further bloodshed." Nolan sighed. "I've prayed over those feelings. Worried over them. And I've come to terms with it. So will you. Zeke Hoskin knows one thing. We're not fighting alone. If he wishes to continue, he'll have to face my brothers and their friends, especially if anyone else is killed. Word will travel fast by sunup."

Sunup. A new day birthing more questions. An ache spread through Aynsley's entire being. How could she face Catherine after running away like a coward? She hadn't meant to hurt her, but the idea of Sara living rocked her foundations and overwhelmed the things she once believed.

Aynsley stroked Nolan's forearm. "Why did Uncle Stewart lie to me?"

He grazed his lips over her forehead. "Reserve judgement until you talk to Catherine. Whatever their reasons were, God promises the truth will set you free. Until then, rest, my love."

Relaxing against him, Aynsley closed her eyes and listened to the steady rhythm of Nolan's heartbeat.

Not many hours later, the murmuring of men's voices woke her. Rubbing her eyes, Aynsley sat up and gained her bearings. Where had Nolan gone? Fatigue shrouded her. From the window, the stars faded in the violet dawn.

Shrugging into her wrapper, she hurried from the room, her bare feet padding down the stairs. In the yard stood two mules hitched to a wagon. Alongside it, Eleazar and Becca spoke with Mr. Kirby and Nolan.

"What's this?" Aynsley swept through the dogtrot, dismay striking her as she summed up the scene. "Why didn't you tell me, Nolan?"

"I found out when I started the chores. I was going to wake you."

"Y'all can't be leaving." The wet dew clung to her toes as her feet touched the ground.

Eleazar's bloodshot eyes, deprived of sleep, implored her to listen. "Zeke knows I shot him. Laid in wait for 'im."

"That's not how it happened."

"It is to him. And it will be to a bunch more. It's best we go."

Clutching Eleazar's arm, she darted a desperate glance at her husband. "Can't you stop him? Persuade him?"

Nolan jammed his hands into his pockets. "Honey, I've reasoned with him, but he's doing what he thinks best."

"Eleazar is right." Mr. Kirby's pained countenance drove the truth home. "Some folks won't care, no matter the facts, and there'll be trouble. Eleazar and Becca would suffer the most."

Desolation, like a sink hole, threatened to drag Aynsley under, but she had to find strength for her beloved friends. She stiffened her spine.

Eleazar grazed a calloused hand over hers, nearly undoing her. "I don't like it no more than you, but it's gotta be this way. I ain't sorry I stopped Zeke, and I'd do it again. I wasn't intending to kill him, but maybe I shoulda. I knew it'd go worse for me and Becca if I did. This way, we got a chance to get out of here."

"Where will you go?"

Becca spoke up. "Last night, while y'all were gone, Miss Catherine wrote a letter and addressed it to a family friend in north Missouri. I have it here." She patted her skirt's pocket. "She knew if Eleazar shot anyone, we'd have to leave. She promised we'd be safe there."

"Will I ever see you both again?"

Doubt clouded Eleazar's eyes, but Becca framed Aynsley's face in her nimble hands.

"Miss Aynsley." Her husky voice quavered. "The Good Book says there's a Promised Land where all God's children go. Someday, we'll see each other again, and we'll walk that shore together, never to be parted no more."

For a long moment, they held each other. When they pulled apart, Becca patted a hand over her heart. "'Till then, I'll carry you here."

Aynsley repeated the motion, but she dared not speak lest she crumble. Stepping beside her, Nolan circled her waist with his arm. He held out his other hand to Eleazar.

"Godspeed, my friend. We'll hold you up in prayer. Thank you for all you've done."

The older man dipped his head. "Glad to be of help."

After helping Becca into the wagon, he rounded the other side and climbed onto the seat. With a slap of the reins, Eleazar urged the mules to go. The wagon jolted forward, and he waved, the shadow of his hat hiding his expression. Becca buried her face into her hands.

"Wait!" Aynsley yelled.

Eleazar tugged the reins, and the wagon halted.

"There's one more thing." Aynsley dashed upstairs. In less than a minute, she returned, sprinting through the dew, the damp hem of her nightgown clinging to her legs.

"Here, Becca." Reaching up, she caught the work-worn hand and nestled her handkerchief inside Becca's palm. "Keep it for me. Always."

Becca's large eyes rounded. "Are you sure?"

"More than anything."

She stroked the stitching, her tears stemming from the outpouring of love. "Whenever I look at it, I'll remember you."

The wagon jerked forward, and once more the strength of Nolan's arm anchored Aynsley.

The smell of freshly baked bread sifted upward through the floor planks from the kitchen and lured open Aynsley's eyelids. Her mind hovered in the mysterious place between waking and sleeping. The afternoon sunlight stretched long beams across the bedroom, and her memories curled open like a flower kissed by the warm rays.

Snuggled by her side, Zadie babbled in her sleep, her haphazard curls lolling across the pillow.

After Eleazar and Becca had departed, Nolan had taken Aynsley upstairs and insisted she rest for the remainder of the day. Zadie had awakened only to eat breakfast and then nestle into bed beside her. She resembled Elnora so much that it stole Aynsley's breath. Lightly brushing a lock from Zadie's cheek, she prayed over her.

Careful not to rouse the child, Aynsley slid out of the bed and dressed. Yesterday hovered like a specter, but she chose to lift a grateful heart to her Heavenly Father for its ending. She loosely plaited her long hair and headed downstairs.

Her mouth watered as the scent of bread thickened. Catherine must be baking, preparing the meals. A mixture of remorse and gratefulness rose, yet Aynsley felt her courage wane as she hesitated outside the open kitchen door.

On the porch sat Mr. Kirby, his brooding stare bouncing from hilltop to hilltop. Sidestepping the doorway, Aynsley joined him. "You could light a wildfire with those eyes."

A wry grin tipped the corners of his mouth. "I'm sorry. It's difficult sitting here when I'd rather be working." He moved his bandaged hands. "No help to anyone around here."

"There's no need for apologies." Aynsley stepped to the porch's edge. "You've helped more than you realize. I pray your hands fully recover."

"They're healing ... slowly. I think they will."

"I'd like to ask you something." She studied him closely. "You've known all this time about Catherine?"

Looking uneasy, Mr. Kirby squirmed. "How could I not?" He slammed his eyes shut. "I didn't mean it the way it sounded. I grew up with her and Stewart. I never liked their decision concerning you, but as a lawyer, I'm not asked to agree. Mind you, I'm the only one outside of the family who knew she was alive."

"Why?"

"It's not my story to tell." He flexed his jaw as though the words begged release.

"You've played a part in it."

He winced. "But you must allow Catherine to explain it."

Aynsley wilted, the thought of facing her mother shriveling up all resolve. She lifted the water pail from its peg. "The truth is a fearsome thing, Mr. Kirby, if you've lived a lie. Excuse me while I take Nolan a fresh drink."

Of course, he was right.

But somehow, she wasn't ready.

CHAPTER THIRTY-SIX

The stilted atmosphere at the supper table had driven everyone to bed early except Nolan. He meandered across the length of the front porch, his thoughts whirling. Recalling the angst on his wife's face made his chest burn.

He longed to help her.

Throughout the meal, Catherine had said nothing, seeming to shrink on her seat while he and Kirby filled the gaps in conversation.

Nolan searched the vast panorama of stars, considering the wisdom holding the universe together. "Father, You are holding Aynsley and our family too. Cause me to know how to help my wife."

Resuming his pace, he continued in prayer for all of them. Imperceptibly, peace settled over him the way a mist unfurls over a field—unnoticed until, all at once, it has blanketed the land.

The Lord would provide healing.

With thanksgiving in his heart, Nolan entered their room and listened to the unhurried breathing of his girls. Not wanting to disturb their slumber, he readied himself for sleep and crawled onto his pallet.

His hip protested against the ungiving floor. Shifting onto his side, Nolan muffled a chuckle. Time for him and Aynsley would come soon enough. He'd waited many a year for her, and he was determined not to rush. Her bruised soul needed space to mend.

Hours later, after the early chores, he and Aynsley returned from the feeding and milking. Careful not to slosh milk from the pail, he stole a glance at her.

"You look a mite rested."

Aynsley gave him a slight smile. "I feel better. How about you?"

"I'm all right." He nodded toward the empty patch where the barn once stood. "It's high time I started rebuilding. Daniel and Jed will help."

"And I'll do all I can as well."

Aynsley followed Nolan into the kitchen where they found Kirby sitting at the table while Catherine wound fresh bandages on his hands.

"'Morning." Nolan set the milk pail aside. "Are you having a lot of pain?"

"A bit," Kirby answered, his mouth taut. "I'll not complain as long as it's healing."

Aynsley fetched four cups and set them beside the coffeepot on the table. While she poured, Nolan lowered himself into a chair. "I'd like to do something different today."

Three curious stares alighted on him. He cleared his throat. "We've come through quite a storm, and I'd like to set aside this day to rest and have a time of devotion to thank God for His faithfulness. How about it?"

Aynsley cut a glance at Catherine. "We need to cook, but I think we could make a lighter meal."

Securing the last bandage, Catherine agreed. "We can."

"I like the idea." Using his unbound thumb, Kirby perched a spoon in his hand and dipped out a sip of coffee before bringing it to his lips.

Nolan's smile encompassed them.

After breakfast, they set chairs under the shade trees while Nolan brought the Bible from the parlor. Holding her doll, Zadie sprawled on the grass in the center, digging her bare toes into the cool, sleek blades.

While the ladies took their seats, a patch of nerves drummed into Nolan. He grappled inwardly for the right words as Kirby led them in prayer. He thought of Aynsley and her thirst for understanding and her inability to comprehend the written word. Her inability colored her approach to life and magnified her fear of confronting the truth. The invisible fetters bound her from everything else within grasp.

The prayer drifted upward, and Nolan sneaked a glance at his wife. She bowed her head and moved her lips in humble petition.

If only Aynsley could see the gift God had created within her.

When Kirby ended the prayer and sat, Nolan thumbed through the Bible until he found First Corinthians. "A lot of folks put stock in things we can see and touch—beauty, wit, talent, and wealth. All those things fade because time corrodes the outward. Beauty diminishes, wit dulls, and talent ceases. Wealth forsakes us when we pass away. For God's children, He bestows qualities that last. Eternal gifts and abilities that get us through times of trouble. Sometimes we are blinded to them, because we can't see past our imperfections."

He'd snagged their attention, especially Aynsley's. She tilted her head to one side as though considering his words. Nolan looked down at the Scripture.

"'Though I speak with the tongues of men and of angels, and have not charity, I am become as sounding brass, or a tinkling cymbal. And though I have the gift of prophecy, and understand all mysteries, and all knowledge; and though I have all faith, so that I could remove mountains, and have not charity, I am nothing.'"

Squinting, Aynsley leaned forward.

While he read the love chapter, he paused occasionally to glimpse her earnest expression. To him, she embodied the charity of those verses, and he yearned for her to realize she possessed the greatest gift of all. He continued.

"'Charity never faileth: but whether there be prophecies, they shall fail; whether there be tongues, they shall cease; whether there be knowledge, it shall vanish away.'"

Conviction strengthened Nolan's voice. "'But when that which is perfect is come, then that which is in part shall be done away. When I was a child, I spake as a child, I understood as a child, I thought as a child: but when I became a man, I put away childish things.'"

Not needing to read the rest, he recited the next lines, words he prayed Aynsley would see. He fastened his gaze onto hers.

"'For now we see through a glass, darkly; but then face to face: now I know in part; but then shall I know even as also I am known.'"

Moisture shimmered in her eyes, and Nolan took courage. "All of us see through a veil. Our sins and imperfections shutter our understanding, but God's light prevails if we allow it. He allows glimpses into His glorious plan for each of us. He exchanges our imperfections through His perfect will in our lives. If He abides in your soul, you have all the abilities you need. Beauty and talent won't rescue you in the day of adversity. Faith in God, the hope of His Salvation, and the power of His love will keep you."

After he ended in prayer, Aynsley drew close. Standing on tiptoes, she whispered into his ear. "I wish I knew what to say, but I can't express it." She patted the spot over her heart. "Thank you."

He grazed her temple with his lips. "Whether you ever read a single word or not, God has granted you His greatest gift: love. Don't dread the truth. You're more than capable of handling it."

Drawing back, Aynsley captured a breath as though taking in his words, her eyes speaking things he understood.

Sunbeams skimmed Aynsley's closed eyelids and warmed her skin as she tipped her head toward the cloudless sky. The breeze twiddled the apple trees and rippled the grass. If she stood motionless and listened, Uncle Stewart's affectionate voice floated past her towards home. Her spirit craved to peer beyond the veil, but she must be content to wait until the Lord restored all things.

The verses, coupled with Nolan's commentary, wove a wonderous picture in Aynsley's thoughts. She offered up her thanksgivings for the Presence and tranquility flowing through her. The load she'd carried loosened its iron cords, liberating her to fully embrace God's infinite love and abandon the notion of a mental deformity.

Though she might never comprehend the written word, He'd given her the capacity to grasp faith, hope, and love. To accept her limitations through grace, confident she was never alone.

The darkened glass existed for a reason few understood. Sometimes, within life's storm, flashes of knowledge illuminated the landscape of hidden truths. Like lightning brightening the mountains for a flicker of time.

To comprehend she was one of countless others standing

at that obscured window brought an unspeakable solace. Best of all, her Savior stood there beside her.

Opening her eyes, Aynsley gazed yonder way at the resting places of her people. Gathering her skirts, she left the protective hedge of the orchard and trekked the path upward. She'd not visited since Elnora's funeral.

The picket gate groaned as she opened it and entered. The bundles of flowers on Elnora's grave had shriveled, their beauty faded. Even yet, Aynsley failed to comprehend how deep-seated jealousy drove Elnora to such treachery. Perhaps she would never discover the answer. Becca had said Elnora's eyes spoke her regrets. Aynsley would hold onto that.

"May I join you?"

At the sound of Catherine's voice, Aynsley swerved around. She fumbled with the buttons near her collar. "I suppose so."

Closing the gate behind her, Catherine swept her glance over the stones, snagging on the one bearing her name. "I had no idea I'd died until I heard about my funeral."

Aynsley frowned. "What?"

"What I told you of Sara and Thad was true. We ran away, disgracing our families. Thad promised to marry me, but he never did."

"Because he died?"

Catherine cringed. "No, because he didn't want it. Of course, I didn't realize that until it was too late. When I discovered I was with child, Thad brought me home in the dead of night and disappeared."

"You mean, he didn't die?" Dizziness assaulted Aynsley.

Twisting her hands, Catherine shook her head. "Father was livid. The next morning, my things were packed, and he sent me to his sister in Missouri. He forbade Stewart to write." Her stare hardened. "Stewart kept contact, though, through

Mitch. On his way to law school, he visited and offered his hand in marriage."

Slamming her eyes shut, Aynsley leaned against a thin maple. "Mr. Kirby?"

"You weren't yet born, but I couldn't do it. By then, I knew he was the better man, but I didn't want him to feel obligated. He continued to intercept and forward letters between me and Stewart. After you were born, Father demanded I find a home for you. He said I couldn't come home otherwise. I couldn't give you up, not to strangers. I loved you so."

The breath wedged in Aynsley's throat.

"When I refused, Father wrote saying I was dead to them and forbade me to return. Likewise, my aunt refused to keep you and said I would have to find another place to live. With a bag of clothes and my baby, I walked several miles—no food, no money. I learned God was my Father on that long walk." Catherine's voice faltered under a tide of emotions. "I finally reached a store. The kind owner and his wife allowed me to live in a room over their establishment, but their business suffered because word spread that they harbored a *loose woman* and her baby."

Trying to absorb the truth, Aynsley scrubbed her forehead with her fingertips. "I cannot imagine."

"They didn't send me away, but they urged me to contact Stewart for his help. You see, our father unexpectedly died. His heart failed. He'd buried Sara only a few days prior to his own death. He'd told folks that I'd died in childbirth. A fitting punishment." Catherine shuddered. "I loved my father dearly. He'd always been kind until then."

Grief struck Aynsley's heart. "How terrible. But to treat you as dead is cruel."

Catherine glanced at her father's headstone, sorrow filling her eyes like a haze. Her expression mirrored the pain of

Aynsley's unresolved conflict with Elnora. Would the emptiness heal?

Aynsley swallowed a rising lump in her throat. "It's difficult when you're left holding the fragments of a broken bond."

"I know you understand. Perhaps Father would've relented once his anger cooled, but he never had the chance. After Stewart received my letter, he came immediately. Since Father had *buried* me in the eyes of friends and neighbors, it seemed fitting to give you a fresh start. I didn't want to bring further disgrace to my brother and his young family by returning— alive. Stewart agreed to adopt and raise you. I could correspond as a cousin—Catherine is my middle name—but I could never return." Tears reddened her eyes. "Giving you up killed a part of me, so I reasoned I might as well be dead."

She pulled a folded sheet of paper from her pocket. "When Mitch informed me of Stewart's death, he sent a letter from him requesting my return, insisting upon your protection. But he also enclosed a message, instructing me to read it to you. May I?"

The air in Aynsley's lungs thinned as she nodded.

"My dear girl,

"When you hear these words, the truth will be clear. I have spent many sleepless nights over my decision allowing Sara to remain buried. All my reasons seem paper-thin as I write this missive. Was my faith so weak that I failed to comprehend the scope of God's grace? Or was my pride wounded over the shame my dear sister brought to our family? Perhaps both.

"I have implored God to forgive my deceit and have taken steps to remedy it. I feel the dangers surrounding us are going to overtake me. My peace with Him is secure, but I must earnestly beg your forgiveness. Never doubt that I loved you, my beloved one.

"I remain your loving uncle,

"Stewart O'Brien"

As though belonging to the same stream, the tears overflowed Catherine's and Aynsley's eyes.

"It's difficult to extend forgiveness to those who are absent, but I need it as much as they do." Catherine skimmed Stewart's cross with her fingertips. "Before he took you, he asked to exchange the handkerchiefs I'd made for us when we were children. He gave me this one ... his." She tugged it from her sleeve. "And I gave him mine. A way to remember each other." Catherine drew close to Aynsley and held it out. "It's rightfully yours."

Crimson and white blurred together as Aynsley's fingers closed over the soft material. She pictured a young, grief-stricken mother granting a memento of lifelong absence for her child to carry. How oft it must have pricked her uncle.

Sara had returned in Stewart's absence, his remaining token now placed in Aynsley's fingers for a lifetime of remembrance. Her heart overflowed. Looking up, she witnessed a light dawning in Sara's blue eyes, shimmering like a sunrise over a turquoise creek.

Both of them were home.

"Mother."

In the quiet shade of the past, mother and daughter found each other.

CHAPTER THIRTY-SEVEN

The home lights of Windy Holler twinkled like golden stars in the twilight. Earlier, after they had spent an hour together, Catherine left Aynsley to contemplate all she'd learned.

Squinting in the dim light, she recognized Nolan's minor limp as he ambled toward her. She closed the gate and hastened to meet him, holding out her hands.

Nolan intertwined their fingers. "And how are you, Mrs. Scottsdale?" His low, husky tone sent a delightful shiver over her.

"I'm better."

"Did you and Catherine have a talk?"

"Oh, Nolan. I must tell you everything."

Arm in arm, they strolled homeward, and she shared every detail. Bending his head closer, he listened, his eyes alert and intent the entire way.

"Has the truth brought healing?" he asked.

"Yes. More than I thought possible."

His hand tightened on hers. "I rejoice with you."

"There's no one else I'd rather rejoice with." Her wispy admission kindled a pleased gleam in his eyes.

"I hope not." The gleam turned into a teasing twinkle before he sobered. Halting, he tipped up her chin, and she lost herself in his gaze. "Aynsley, I love you. Always have and will forever."

Her chest hitched, the wonder of it astonishing. Her words, imprisoned for so long, broke free. "And I love you."

Nolan lowered his head, then shot a glance at the breezeway. "I'm forgetting myself. We're not quite alone."

With a groan, he whisked behind a tree and crushed her to him. Aynsley's arms circled his neck. Together, they expressed their fervor, joy bubbling between them.

Raising his head a fraction, Nolan framed her face. "Speaking of share, the floor in our room is a mite uncomfortable." The smile in his voice was unmistakable.

Aynsley fingered his collar, feigning innocence. "Oh, do you need a few more quilts?"

"Not exactly, Mrs. Scottsdale."

"Mayhap a cot instead?"

Tunneling his fingers into her hair, Nolan stole a swift, firm kiss that thrilled all the way to her toes. He touched his forehead to hers. "Mayhap not."

"I think we can work something out. After all, enough is enough."

"I couldn't agree more."

When he sought her lips once again, a tiny giggle sputtered from the other side of the tree, breaking them apart. A golden-headed culprit skipped around the trunk.

"Zadie Charlotte." Aynsley's face tingled while she smoothed her hair into place.

"You rascal." Nolan swooped her into his arms. "Sneakin' up on folks is rude in some parts."

For an answer, Zadie squealed in delight, and they both laughed. Nolan boosted her onto his shoulders. "We've got our hands full with this one."

"Blessedly so." Aynsley took Nolan's hand, and they continued to the cabin where their future awaited.

A NOTE FROM THE AUTHOR

The Civil War ravaged the Ozarks. Although the majority of the fighting occurred in other well-known places around the country, Confederate and Union guerillas swept through the hills, killing people and pillaging whatever they pleased. These savage men were soldiers in name only. People referred to the Confederate guerillas as Bushwhackers, and Union guerillas were called Jayhawkers.

Bloody Ozarks by G.W. Johnson shares heartrending stories of Union loyalists in Arkansas, but no family was left untouched by the indiscriminate killers. Most were caught in the middle of the violence.

The incident of Kirby's hands being scorched is based on an actual event in *Bloody Ozarks*, except it happened to a woman whose feet were burned when she refused to disclose her husband's whereabouts to the bushwhackers.

Let's talk a little about Aynsley.

Word blindness was first coined by German Professor of Medicine Adolph Kussmaul in 1877, which is twelve years after this story. Though his premise was incorrect, he opened the door for future studies of this condition. Today, we know it as dyslexia.

To understand a little of Aynsley's challenges, I read *The Gift of Dyslexia: Why Some of the Smartest People Can't Read ... and How They Can Learn* by Ronald D. Davis, who is dyslexic himself.

I was fascinated by his study. He claims that most dyslexics have no internal dialog like most people. Instead, they think in pictures. The process is vivid, complex, and instantaneous.

As a writer, how was I going to convey Aynsley's thoughts? How would readers get to know her otherwise? Thoughts are crucial to storytelling. I decided to show Aynsley's as much as possible through pictures. Sometimes I couldn't find a way to express her internal dialog except through words. In those instances, I expressed them as shortly and sweetly as possible with the idea I was interpreting the pictures in her mind. Other times, I had Aynsley verbalize her thoughts aloud when she was alone.

The ridicule and humiliation she experienced is real. Many have suffered taunts from people, family, and teachers alike, especially when dyslexia was not widely known or understood. One of the things I loved about Davis's book is his emphasis that dyslexia is a gift rather than a disability. He explores those reasons, some of which I endeavored to show through Aynsley. If you know anyone who might benefit from this book, I highly recommend it.

I'm by no means an expert, so I beg the reader's pardon for any creative license I took with Aynsley. She was challenging and so rewarding to create, and I believe she'll remain one of my favorite characters.

ABOUT CANDACE WEST

CANDACE WEST was born in the Mississippi delta to a young minister and his wife. She grew up in small-town Arkansas and graduated from the University of Arkansas at Monticello. At twelve years old, she wrote her first story, "Following Prairie River," during a long car trip to Colorado. The writing spark has not dimmed since.

In 2018, she published her debut novel *Lane Steen*. In 2021, her novel, *Valley of Shadows*, was a Selah Award finalist. By weaving page-turning, entertaining stories, Candace shares the Gospel and encourages her readers. She currently lives in Arkansas with her husband and their son along with two dogs and three bossy cats.

BOOK CLUB QUESTIONS

1. Do you think Stewart O'Brien's stipulations in his will were fair to Aynsley? Why or why not?
2. Aynsley is dyslexic, which no one in 1865 understood. Do you know anyone who has faced similar challenges? In what ways are those challenges similar or different than Aynsley's?
3. Why do you think Elnora turned Zadie against Aynsley?
4. Deception causes a terrible misunderstanding between Aynsley and Nolan. Has deception ever driven a wedge between you and a loved one?
5. Why do you think Aynsley tends to fear the truth? How do her insecurities hold her back?
6. The Hoskins resort to cruel tactics in order to drive Eleazar and Becca from Windy Hollow. Do you agree with Eleazar's decision? Why or why not?
7. How does Aynsley win Zadie's trust?
8. Aynsley's condition hinders her from fully embracing herself and others. How does Nolan and her faith in God help her overcome?

9. What do Sara's and Stewart's handkerchiefs represent to Aynsley? Why are they important to her? Do you have a keepsake that is significant to you?

10. Stewart O'Brien is the driving force that brings Catherine and Aynsley together? What do you think of his devotion to these ladies?

TITLES BY CANDACE WEST

THE MOSAIC COLLECTION: NOVELS
Windy Hollow Series
Through the Lettered Veil

THE MOSAIC COLLECTION: ANTHOLOGY STORIES
"A Garland of Grace"
(*A Star Will Rise: A Mosaic Christmas Anthology II*)
"Forever Mine"
(*Song of Grace: Stories to Amaze the Soul*)

VALLEY CREEK REDEMPTION SERIES
Lane Steen
Valley of Shadows
Dogwood Winter

THANK YOU FOR READING!

We hope you enjoyed reading *Through the Lettered Veil* by Candace West. If you did, please consider leaving a short review on Amazon, Goodreads, or BookBub. Positive reviews and word-of-mouth recommendations honor an author and help other readers to find quality Christian fiction to read.

Thank you so much!

If you'd like to receive information about The Mosaic Collection's new releases and writing news, please subscribe to *Grace & Glory*, Mosaic's monthly newsletter.

How do you persevere when you have no more will to fight?

Jennifer and Chad Taylor had dreamed of opening a coffee and cocoa shop since before they said, "I do." When Chad is sent to prison for murder despite claiming innocence, that dream —along with their family—is shattered.

After years of fighting for Chad's release, Jennifer finally breaks free from her shame, anger, and hopelessness, and forges ahead with the dream the two of them once shared. With the help of their college-aged twins, she begins to move forward.

Without Chad.

When their lawyer arrives with news of evidence that may prove Chad's innocence, a strange mixture of emotions overtakes her. Does she want Chad to return home? He isn't the same man he once was, and she certainly isn't the same woman. She's worked hard to piece the remnants of their family back together, and his coming home could fracture the family once again.

It all comes down to one question. She loves her husband enough to fight for his release from prison, but does she love him enough to fight for their marriage?

bit.ly/BrokenTogetherMosaic